D0915859

Shooting Star

Cynthia Bates

James Lorimer & Company Ltd., Publishers
Toronto, 2001

James Lorimer & Company Ltd. acknowledges the support of the Ontario Arts Council. We acknowledge the support of the Government of Canada through the Book Publishing Industry Development Program (BPIDP) for our publishing activities. We acknowledge the support of the Canada Council for the Arts for our publishing program.

Cover illustration: Greg Ruhl

Cataloguing in Publication Data

Bates, Cynthia, 1950–
   Shooting star

(Sports stories; 46)
ISBN 1-55028-727-3 (bound)   ISBN 1-55028-726-5 (pbk.)

I. Title. II. Series: Sports stories (Toronto, Ont.); 46.

PS8553.A8263S56 2001   jC813'.54   C00-933218-9
PZ7.B473Sh 2001

James Lorimer & Company Ltd.,
Publishers
35 Britain Street
Toronto, Ontario
M5A 1R7

Distributed in the United States by:
Orca Book Publishers
P.O. Box 468
Custer, WA USA
98240–0468

Printed and bound in Canada.

Contents

To Susan,
the dearest of friends,
better than a sister.

1

The Offer

"U nreasonable," Quyen Ha muttered crossly as she left the office of her gym teacher and coach, Ms. Bradford.

"What's unreasonable?" came a friendly voice from behind. Quyen's best friend, Amelie Blair, had somehow managed to approach her, without Quyen realizing she was there.

"Not, 'what?' 'Who?'" Quyen replied, continuing her usual quick-paced steps in the direction of her locker, located on the first floor of Nellie McClung Middle School in Ottawa's Centretown neighbourhood.

"Okay, okay! Then 'who'?" Amelie persisted. "Slow down, for crying out loud! Jeez, you'd think you were training for cross-country!"

Quyen arrived at her locker near the music room and turned to face Amelie. Quyen did not often lose her temper, but she was angry now and she felt her face flushed with it. Outwardly maintaining her composure, she regarded her friend evenly.

"That's very funny, Ammi," Quyen said, clearly unamused. "The training part, I mean."

Amelie's perpetual grin disappeared. "Oops," she said. "Did I say something wrong?"

Quyen turned back to her locker and began to work the combination. "Of course not," she relented. Amelie was the most kind-hearted person Quyen knew. Despite her own foul mood, Quyen couldn't bear to see the hurt look on her friend's face. "I just went to see Ms. Bradford like you and Jill suggested. You know, about cross-country?"

Amelie nodded, her mop of brown curls bouncing vigorously. "Uh-oh," she said, suddenly still. "Don't tell me she turned down the idea!"

It was still before eight o'clock in the morning and the hallways were empty. Within ten minutes, there would be boys and girls heading for the two gyms located at the opposite end of the L-shaped corridor from where Quyen and Amelie stood. Tryouts for the school's grade eight volleyball teams were starting that morning and, as the McClung teams were defending provincial champions and bronze medallists, excitement was high among all the hopefuls.

Quyen's slender shoulders sagged a little as she again faced her friend. "She said she couldn't make any exceptions — 'not even for you, Quyen,'" Quyen mimicked.

"But you weren't asking to be excused from training, right? You just wanted to train at lunch," Amelie persisted.

Ms. Bradford, head coach of the McClung Cougars girls' sports team, had a firm rule: all girls who wanted to make the volleyball and basketball teams had to participate in cross-country training in order to get into top shape.

"I didn't even get to that!" Quyen replied, hanging her sweater on a hook inside the locker. "I was just trying to explain my situation, and as soon as she heard me say that I couldn't get to the park three mornings a week, she freaked out! She started going on about 'no exceptions' and 'don't let the team down' and a bunch of other stuff. I couldn't get a word in!"

"I know what you mean," Amelie said sympathetically. "Sometimes Ms. Bradford doesn't listen very well, but she has been great to me since I came to McClung last year."

"You're right, Ammi," Quyen conceded. "I was pretty impressed with how Ms. Bradford got you involved with the team right away when you first came. And she was super understanding about the whole Anna thing."

"Definitely," Amelie agreed. "Maybe you just caught her at a bad time."

"Well, this was the wrong time to be a bad time as far as I'm concerned," Quyen said, shaking her head. Her long, straight, black hair swung across the tops of her shoulders. She closed her locker, having retrieved a paperback novel.

"What are you doing?" Amelie asked. "The tryout starts in five minutes! Get your gym stuff."

"Ammi, I'm not trying out," Quyen replied gently, as if she thought her friend couldn't handle the information. In fact, Amelie was so sensitive, Quyen was sure her friend would have a hard time with Quyen's decision not to play.

"Of course you are!" Amelie said, a trace of panic in her voice.

Quyen started to walk toward the near stairwell, away from the direction of the gyms. "No," she said firmly. "I'm not. I told Ms. Bradford I wouldn't be playing on any school teams this year." She turned her head in Amelie's direction before pushing through the double doors to the stairs. "Sorry, Ammi. I'll see you at lunch." She opened the doors and walked through, leaving her friend standing with her mouth hanging open in disbelief.

* * *

At lunch, Quyen joined her friends, as usual, at their favourite table in a corner of the crowded lunch room. A cool September rain had started to fall in the middle of the morning, so the space was filled to capacity.

Quyen's friends, her teammates throughout their grade seven year, were already seated when she arrived. Usually relaxed and cheerful — especially at lunch — today they looked serious and concerned. As soon as they saw Quyen, everyone began to speak at once.

"Whoa, hold on!" Quyen said, holding up a hand to quiet them. She allowed the smallest smile in an effort to reassure her friends. "I didn't understand a word anyone said!"

Daphne Jones, her green eyes flashing, stood authoritatively as if to preside over the situation. At just under five feet, Daphne knew it was the only way to make sure that she got the attention of the other girls.

"Quyen," Daphne said, a hint of indignation in her tone. "If you're not going to play on the team, then I'm not either."

"What are you talking about, Daph?" Mei-lin said. "You didn't want to play anyway."

Mei-lin was even smaller than Daphne, a quiet, soft-spoken girl who had arrived in Canada from Vietnam as a young child. She and Quyen had known each other since preschool.

"Well, now I won't for sure!" Daphne replied petulantly. As she nodded her head for emphasis, her brilliant red hair loosened itself further from the confines of an already messy ponytail. "Ms. Bradford can't get away with doing that to Quyen. Anyway," she added, "it was the cross-country that I didn't want to do, not volleyball!"

"Why don't we wait and hear what Quyen has to say," said Jill, a pretty golden-haired girl. As usual, she was clad in jeans and an older brother's cast-off sweatshirt.

"Good idea," Amelie agreed, speaking for the first time.

Quyen sighed, then sat down at the table and took out her lunch, a neat little sandwich and a small bag of fresh vegetables. She drained her container of orange juice before starting her explanation.

"Look, you guys," she began, "it's simple. I went to Ms. Bradford to ask her if I could do the running at lunchtime. But I guess I started out with the wrong information because, as soon as I said I couldn't get to the park in the morning, she cut me off. 'Blah, blah, blah,' she goes, and, in the meantime, I'm getting madder and madder."

"So, in other words," Jill said, "you didn't even get a chance to ask the question."

"That's how it went," Quyen replied. "But the bad part is that when she finally let me talk, I was so angry I just said, 'Fine. I won't play on *any* teams this year.'"

"That's *so* not you, Quinnie," Mei-lin observed, calling Quyen by her seldom-used pet name.

"Exactly," added Daphne. "I've never seen you really lose your temper since grade two when Mark Melvin took your shoes and hid them."

"I remember that!" laughed Jill. "The whole school heard Quyen giving Mark you-know-what!"

"Well, *that* explains why Mark Melvin is so strange," Amelie offered, joining the laughter. "Quyen probably scared him permanently into weirdness."

"You guys are right," Quyen said quietly, chewing on a carrot stick as she reflected. "I'm not myself these days."

Just then, Pauline Duval approached the girls' table. "Hey, gang, what's up?" she asked.

"Not much, Pauline," Daphne answered as the others smiled at the young woman. Pauline had immigrated to Canada from Haiti as a child. She'd discovered basketball at McClung under Ms. Bradford's encouragement and had become so good at the game that she'd gone on to play five years of university basketball. Now she was a volunteer coach at McClung while attending teachers' college.

"Quyen, have you got a minute?" Pauline asked.

Quyen rose from the table, picked up the remains of her lunch and smoothly shot the small wadded bundle into a garbage can four metres away. She glanced at the supervising teacher, whose back was turned, then breathed a sigh of relief when she saw Mr. Friesen, the school caretaker, enter the lunch room just as her refuse landed safely in the receptacle.

Quyen followed Pauline into the hallway and in the direction of Ms. Bradford's office.

"Hold on," Quyen said, stopping. "Where are we going?"

"Don't worry, she's gone out for a run," Pauline replied, anticipating Quyen's objection.

"In the rain? That woman is a fanatic!"

"No," Pauline said, unlocking the gym office door. "The rain's let up. I think Ms. Bradford needed to de-stress."

"Hmm," Quyen muttered. "She *definitely* needs to de-stress!"

"Yeah, I heard about what happened this morning." Pauline sat down at the desk and indicated a chair for Quyen. "You know, I think Ms. Bradford was pretty upset."

"Well, that's *her* problem. She didn't even wait to hear what I had to say!"

"You know Ms. Bradford, Quyen. She's human. Sometimes she doesn't listen too well. I'm sure if you just explained ..."

"No way, Pauline." Quyen was adamant despite a faint recognition in the back of her mind that she, too, was being unreasonable.

"Wow, something sure is bugging you, Quyen. You don't usually react like this."

Quyen was silent. The things that were on her mind were *her* business. Only Amelie had any idea of what was going on in Quyen's life to make her so testy and even she didn't know the whole story. *Of course*, Quyen thought, *that's only because I don't know the whole story.*

"Okay, Quyen, never mind," Pauline said finally. "Listen, I'm coaching a bantam team with the Shooting Stars this year."

"The Shooting Stars Basketball Club?" Now Quyen was interested.

"Uh-huh. You've heard of Coach Andrews?" Pauline asked.

"Who hasn't? Amelie and Jill raved about what a great coach he was after their March Break basketball camp last year." Quyen recalled her friends' enthusiasm with a smile. Amelie in particular had returned to her McClung team from the camp with increased self-confidence. After having been bullied at her previous school, Amelie had started at McClung stung by the harrowing experience. Quyen was still sometimes amazed to think that someone with Amelie's sunny, outgoing personality could have been reduced to the timid girl she first encountered in January.

"It's true. Coach Andrews is probably one of the top coaches in the province," Pauline was explaining. "Even my university coach at Windsor knew who he was and had a lot of good things to say about him. Anyway, he's asked me to be his assistant coach this year. There was no way I was going to turn down *that* opportunity."

"Awesome," Quyen replied. "You'll be great!"

"What I was wondering," Pauline said, "was if you might be interested in trying out. That is, if you meant it about not playing on school teams this year. Which, by the way," she added, "I would prefer not to believe."

"Oh, I meant it," Quyen said, sounding like she wasn't so sure she meant it at all. "But I don't know about playing with a club team. That's a big time commitment, isn't it?"

"Truthfully?" Pauline said. "Yes. There will be two practices a week at Ashwood Academy where Coach Andrews teaches. Wednesday evenings and, a little later on, Sunday afternoons. Once the season begins, we'll play on Saturdays twice a month and occasionally spend weekends at away tournaments."

"Holy Smokes! That's even more than I thought," Quyen said. "Thanks for asking, Pauline, but I really don't know how I'd manage that."

"Well," said Pauline, clearly disappointed. "Think about it. Maybe ask your folks. Tryouts start this Wednesday."

"I'll think about it, Pauline," Quyen said, standing up. "But it's just too much. My parents would never go for it."

As she left the gym office, Quyen felt herself close to tears. But crying was something she had given up in grade five and she wasn't about to start again over her muddled sports life. No, if she were going to cry over something, it would be about what was going on at home.

Now that, Quyen thought, *is a situation worthy of tears.*

2

As Expected

That evening, Quyen and her sister, Ming, shared clean-up chores in the kitchen after dinner. Ming was exactly a year younger than Quyen and, except for an eight-centimetre difference in height, closely resembled her older sister. Both girls had perfectly straight jet-black hair, although Ming kept hers shorter, just below the ears, with bangs, while Quyen's hair fell to the tops of her shoulders and her longer bangs were brushed to the side. So striking was their delicate beauty that they frequently attracted the unwanted stares of strangers in public. Their parents had been approached more than once to consider modelling careers for the girls, requests they had emphatically declined. The sisters were as close as if they were twins, and they rarely argued. Lately, they'd had more cause than usual to seek out each other's thoughts.

Mrs. Ha had excused herself following dinner, saying that she felt a little tired and was going to lie down for a while. This was now a familiar routine to the girls, although occasionally their mother surprised them by reverting to having the girls take turns tidying the kitchen with her. Quyen missed the regular opportunities to catch her mother up on what was happening at school and with her friends.

Quyen and Ming did not expect to see their mother again before breakfast and, as they cleaned, Quyen started explaining to her sister what had happened earlier that day at school between herself and Ms. Bradford.

"Oh, Quinnie, that's terrible!" Ming responded. "And after you helped McClung win bronze medals at the provincials last year! You'd think Ms. Bradford would do anything to have you on the team again this year."

"Apparently not," Quyen replied with a shrug, clearing the last of the dishes from the table. "Anyway, I said what I said and I'm not taking it back."

Ming was quiet. She seemed to know better than to try to change Quyen's mind once it had been made up.

"How did you find our mother this evening?" Ming asked, changing the subject. She rinsed a bowl and passed it to Quyen to put in the dishwasher.

"About the same as she's been for weeks, I guess," Quyen replied. "Quiet, preoccupied ..."

"What's that?"

"Preoccupied? Oh, it just means that her thoughts seem to be somewhere other than ... well, *here*," Quyen explained. She poured powdered detergent into a little compartment inside the dishwasher door and snapped its lid shut before closing the machine.

"Hm-hmm," Ming agreed. "That sounds right. She always seems to be daydreaming, but not, you know, *happy* daydreaming."

"What about Father? Did he seem in a good mood to you?" Quyen wondered.

"It's very hard to say anymore. Sometimes I see him smiling at nothing but, when I start to talk to him, he's actually quite crabby and cross," Ming replied. "Why?"

Quyen tossed a damp cloth to Ming. "Here, wipe the table, please. I'm going to put on some water for tea."

"Why did you ask about Father, Quyen?" Ming repeated.

"Oh, I was just wondering if it would be a good time to ask him about whether or not I could try out for the Shooting Stars basketball team."

"The Shooting Stars!" Ming cried. "*Now* I understand why you're not upset about giving up school teams."

"Of course I'm upset," Quyen said matter-of-factly. "But what's done is done. I will have to look into other ways of playing sports this year."

Quyen poured tea and the girls sat back down at the table.

"Gosh, Quyen, I don't know how you can stay calm. With our parents behaving so mysteriously, and you quitting the teams at McClung, I know *I* would be feeling kind of — I don't know — stressed."

"Well, I can't tell you I'm *not* stressed," Quyen said with a sigh, "but I don't see what's to be gained by getting all hysterical about things."

"Okay, so what about the Shooting Stars? A girl in my class has played with them for two years and she loves it!"

"Really?" Quyen replied. "It was Pauline who talked to me about it today. She said I should ask my parents, but I figured there probably wasn't much point."

"Not much point to what?"

Quyen turned at the sound of her father's stern voice. He was standing in the kitchen doorway, a frown creasing his already deeply furrowed brow.

"Oh, Father, I didn't realize you were there," Quyen said. She managed to mask the distress in her voice at having been caught off guard.

"Would you like some tea, Father?" Ming asked, rising to get it.

"No thank you," Mr. Ha replied, then turned again to Quyen. "You were saying?"

Quyen cleared her throat unnecessarily, but her voice was strong and steady as she began to explain. "Father, I had a ...

a discussion today with Ms. Bradford. We were not able to come to an agreement on a training program for me to follow in order to play on the volleyball team. I told her that I would not be participating on the team this year."

Mr. Ha nodded thoughtfully as he considered this information. "Then you will have more time for your studies. Am I right?"

Quyen glanced at Ming who looked as if she were dying to jump into the conversation, but was so far resisting the temptation.

"Well, actually," Quyen continued, "Ms. Bradford's assistant, Pauline, asked me today if I would like to try out for a position on the club basketball team that she helps coach."

"What do you mean, 'club'?" Mr. Ha asked.

"It's a team that has players from different schools on it and they practise in the evening and play on weekends," Quyen explained, knowing, as she listened to herself, that her father would never go for it.

"Evenings? Weekends?" he repeated, wonderingly. "And where are these practices, at your school?"

"No," Quyen replied, "at Ashwood Academy. It's a private school in Rockway." She thought that at least her father might be impressed with the prestigious neighbourhood in which the school was located.

"You were right," Mr. Ha said finally, "about there being no point. You do not need to be running around like a boy playing sports when you can be working on your school assignments and helping your mother at home." With that, he turned abruptly and disappeared down the hallway.

Quyen looked at Ming's sorrowful expression and knew that, at that moment, she could not say a word to her sister, for fear of breaking down.

3

Annoyed but Interested

"Not a chance, Pauline, forget it!" Quyen said calmly. "Let's go, Ammi," she added, tossing her hair as she turned on her heel and walked briskly towards the doors.

Quyen and Amelie quickly exited the Ashwood Academy gym. The girls were now only vaguely aware of the rich surroundings they so admired upon entering the school earlier that Saturday afternoon. Heavy, dark wood beams framed ivory walls that held photographs of former teams and illustrious individuals whose presence had once graced the century-old private school.

Three weeks had passed since Quyen had withdrawn from participation on school teams. She had not even told Amelie how restless she was feeling from the lack of activity and competition. She knew her friend would only start nagging her to speak to Ms. Bradford again. But it had been Amelie, not Pauline, who had talked Quyen into coming to watch the first Shooting Stars exhibition game. On the unusually warm Saturday morning in late September Pauline had driven the girls to Ashwood, barely concealing her excitement over the Stars' first game. She was obviously proud of her role as the assistant coach.

"Hey, wait a minute," Pauline called, having followed the girls out. "What's this all about, anyway?"

Quyen slowed down once she reached the hallway. She waited for Pauline to catch up.

"Are you trying to tell me you didn't know Anna Archer is on that team?" Quyen demanded in disbelief.

"Well, of course I knew she's on the team! I'm the assistant coach!" Pauline was obviously as exasperated with the conversation as Quyen. "What's the big deal?"

Amelie turned to Quyen, whose dark eyes were bright with annoyance. "Quyen," she said, "Ms. Bradford must not have told Pauline everything that happened with Anna."

Pauline looked distressed. "Look, girls, I *do* remember that there was some kind of conflict between you and Anna, but I had no idea it was so serious! In any case, I'm sorry, but right now I've got to get back into the gym. The game's going to start any minute. Please put whatever it is aside for the moment and come watch."

"It's okay, Pauline," Amelie said. "You go ahead. We'll be there in a minute."

Quyen and Amelie watched in silence as Pauline hurried back into the gym. Even rushing, the young woman moved with an athletic grace unexpected in someone so small and muscular.

"Why is Pauline coaching this team, anyway?" Quyen asked her friend irritably. "Doesn't she have enough to do coaching our school team?"

"Guess not," Amelie replied, shrugging. "*You're* the one who told me that coaching the Shooting Stars and working with Coach Andrews was a great opportunity for her. That team travels all over the province and even into Quebec and the States, you know."

Quyen did not respond.

"Quyen?" Amelie pressed.

"Sorry, what was that?" Quyen asked, her thoughts clearly somewhere else.

"Listen, Quyen, I know things haven't been going all that well at home but you've really clammed up lately! What's happening? I've never seen you so crabby and ... and *deranged!*"

Quyen laughed in spite of herself. "I hope you mean 'distracted'," she said, then heaved a huge sigh. "You're right. I'm not myself. Maybe 'deranged' *is* the right word." After a moment's pause she continued. "Okay. If you don't mind being in the same gym with Anna, we might as well go back in. We're going to have to wait for Pauline to drive us home anyway."

"Look, I can handle being in the same gym with Anna if you can handle opening up about what's going on. Are things worse with your parents?"

The two girls re-entered the gym and made their way up into the bleachers. They settled themselves onto the hard wooden seats as the ball was tossed to start the game between the Ottawa Shooting Stars and the Gloucester Badgers. Pauline had explained that the Badgers were undefeated in regional play during their previous two years and were predicting a provincial championship for themselves this season.

"Check it out, Ammi," Quyen said, mesmerized by the action below, in spite of her black mood. "Are they ever good!"

"Yeah, they move the ball pretty well, all right."

"Pretty well!" Quyen exclaimed. "You can hardly see it! Now that's my kind of passing."

Amelie laughed. "Remember what a hard time everyone on the Cougars had trying to handle your passes at first?"

"Hmm ... yeah, but we had fun, didn't we?"

"You bet," Amelie answered wistfully. "I don't know how we'll manage if you don't play with us this year, Quyen."

Quyen, engrossed in the game, did not reply. She had stuck with her decision not to play on any school teams despite emotional pleas from her friends to straighten out the misunderstanding with Ms. Bradford over morning training. Quyen lived quite far from the school and her father would neither drive her to school early nor permit her to take public transportation.

Within a few days, Quyen had desperately regretted her stubbornness, wondering how she would survive the year without sports. "Pig-headedness is not a virtue," she'd muttered to Amelie when they'd discussed the situation.

Amelie had tried to counsel her friend. "All you have to do is go back to Ms. Bradford and explain ..."

"It's not a virtue," Quyen repeated, interrupting. "But it's not as shameful as begging and pleading."

The look of determination on Quyen's face at that moment had discouraged Amelie from pursuing the matter any further.

* * *

By the end of the first quarter, the Badgers had a sixteen-point lead. During the time out, Quyen turned to her friend. "Ammi," she said, "I know you're disappointed I'm not playing with the Cougars this year — I am too! But I couldn't go back on what I told Ms. Bradford ..."

"You're so stubborn!" Amelie interrupted. "You know darned well Ms. Bradford would take you on the volleyball team in a flash if you'd just explain to her why you can't make those morning practices."

"You think I didn't try?" Quyen replied. "She wouldn't let me get a word in edgewise. Anyway, I'm not going to tell her personal family stuff — that's not her business!"

"No, I guess not," Amelie said softly. "Lately, you don't even tell me."

"Oh, Ammi, I'm not trying to keep anything from you," Quyen said, seeing her friend's concern. "There's nothing more than I've already told you. It's just that things aren't getting any better!"

"Do you still think your mom might be sick?" Amelie asked cautiously.

"I don't know what to think! She spends so much time in her room. Ming and I can hear her crying sometimes. And my father is like a zombie! Either he's at work or he's in his office at home on the telephone or writing letters. He won't tell us anything, just, 'Everything is fine, daughters. Do your homework.'"

The game had started again and the girls returned their attention to the action on the floor. The Badgers were firmly in control of the game, increasing their lead steadily until halftime, leaving the hapless Stars down by a score of 28–6.

"Jeez," remarked Amelie, "the only points the Stars have scored have been on free throws!"

"Hm-hmm," Quyen agreed thoughtfully. "Their passes are terrible. They've turned over the ball on every possession but a couple. Even if Coach Andrews is as good as everyone says, he'll have his work cut out for him this season without a decent point guard."

"Which could be *you*, Quyen," Amelie ventured cautiously. "You know darned well Pauline brought us to this game so you would see how much the Shooting Stars could use you."

"Yeah," Quyen replied, a small smile curving the ends of her lips. "She thinks she's so clever."

"Actually, Quyen," Amelie said hesitantly, "Pauline told *me* that Coach Andrews was desperate for a good point guard and I sort of, well, you know … *suggested* that, well, *maybe* you *might*, just *possibly*, be interes—"

"You didn't!" Quyen exclaimed, amused. Then, in a more serious tone. "Why, I never would have guessed that you'd try to manipulate me …"

Quyen stopped when she saw the look of horror on her friend's face. "Relax, Ammi, I'm just kidding! It wasn't hard to figure out that there was *some* kind of ulterior motive when you and Pauline were so determined to get me to this game."

"Whew!" Amelie exhaled, "I thought you were really mad."

"I'm sorry, Amelie. Maybe playing with the Shooting Stars would get my mind off things. But my father was pretty firm, to say the least," Quyen paused a moment, reflecting. "Anyway, what about Anna Archer? Did you notice how she glares at us whenever she's on the bench, which, thank heavens for her team, isn't often?"

"I noticed, all right," Amelie replied. "But you can handle Anna, Quyen. You'd look right through her. Me? She gives me the shivers. There are just too many bad memories ..."

Quyen nodded thoughtfully. "No wonder, Ammi. It doesn't look like her attitude has changed, either. Do you suppose she goes to school here at Ashwood now?"

"I did hear over the summer that she wasn't going back to Queen Vic. And her mother could certainly afford to send her here!" Amelie replied.

Quyen silently reviewed the circumstances that had brought Amelie to McClung in the middle of the previous school year. Amelie had started grade seven at Queen Victoria Junior High with her best friend of several years, a girl named Jessie. But during the preceding summer, while Amelie was visiting her grandparents in Prince Edward Island, Jessie had met and made friends with Anna Archer at a summer camp. Anna had taken an inexplicable dislike to Amelie from the moment they were introduced and had set about making Amelie's life miserable at Queen Vic.

Jealousy, Quyen thought. Anna had wanted Jessie's friendship exclusively. Quyen figured that, despite her good looks and outward show of confidence, Anna Archer was, for some reason, too insecure to share her new friend with some-one as well-liked as Amelie. From what Amelie had told her, Anna had demonstrated considerable skill in manipulating others to believe outrageous lies about Amelie, and Amelie's life had gradually become an unbearable nightmare.

Quyen felt no desire whatsoever to know Anna well enough to figure out what had made her so hateful.

* * *

The second half of the game was a little better than the first. Quyen was impressed to see that Coach Andrews and Pauline seemed to have made some successful adjustments, enabling the Shooting Stars to score a few baskets while stepping up their defense to prevent the glut of Badger scoring witnessed in the first half. The final score was 44–18.

When the coaches finished meeting with the exhausted Stars and the players had retired to the locker room, Pauline waved Quyen and Amelie over to the bench.

"Quyen," Pauline said, "I'd like you to meet Mr. Andrews, coach of the Shooting Stars. Amelie, I think you already know Coach Andrews from camp last March, right?"

Amelie smiled and nodded shyly as Quyen shook hands with the coach.

"Hey, Ammi, good to see you again," Coach Andrews said. "Quyen, I've heard a lot about you and I had a chance to see you play last spring. Glad to meet you. Sorry we couldn't put on a better show for you girls today. The Badgers not only play better than we do right now, they know how to psyche us out so we end up playing worse against them than any other team!"

The girls smiled at the coach's easy analysis of his team's performance.

"We're down a couple of team members this season. Two of our stronger players — twin sisters — moved away unexpectedly. Both of you would be great additions to the Stars' roster," Mr. Andrews continued. "Amelie, I remember your skills and your ability to handle the post position very well."

"Sorry, Mr. Andrews, I've got enough going on with school teams and trying to keep up with homework," Amelie replied. "But thanks for asking."

"Quyen? I saw you play in the McClung tournament," the Stars coach said, "You've got just what we're looking for. Speed, smarts, skills ... and you know how to keep your cool. Great height, too. That's a real bonus in a point guard. What about giving it a try?"

"I don't know, Mr. Andrews," Quyen said, "I've got a lot to keep up with as well."

"Would you at least think about it? Pauline can fill you in on whatever you need to know. Next practice is Wednesday. We'd love to see you."

"I'll think about it," Quyen said, nodding thoughtfully. "Thanks."

On the drive home, Amelie and Pauline chatted pleasantly about the McClung Cougars' upcoming volleyball season and provincial championships. Quyen sat quietly, listening to them for awhile. She was pleased that Amelie would be playing at the Provincials this year, even though Quyen would not. Quyen wondered once again how Anna had succeeded in turning Jessie and Amelie's other friends against her. Since arriving at McClung, Amelie had made friends quickly and easily and had become a popular leader within the girls' athletic program. Quyen knew only too well, however, how badly the previous experiences sometimes still haunted her usually optimistic friend.

Preoccupied with Amelie and Anna, Quyen's thoughts were inevitably led to basketball. What, she wondered, was the possibility that she could persuade her father to let her play? Not great, she knew. But, no matter how hard she resisted, an image kept surfacing in her mind: herself in a black and white Shooting Stars uniform, firing blistering passes to Anna Archer in the post.

4

The Tension Mounts

Pauline dropped Amelie at her east-end Ottawa home before starting into an earnest discussion with Quyen about the merits of being a member of the Shooting Stars.

"You'd love it, Quyen. You really would. I mean, I know that was a terrible game for you to watch, but I really wanted you to see how badly the team needs a good point guard — someone who can handle the ball with confidence, who's coachable and not easily intimidated."

Quyen, generally uncomfortable with compliments, was flattered by Pauline's praise. Pauline was someone whose opinion she respected. "I just don't know, Pauline. My father is very busy these days. I know he wouldn't be too enthusiastic about driving me to all the practices and games." To ensure that Pauline understood the obstacles in her way, she added, "Besides, he says that all these extracurricular activities interfere with school and homework."

"Quyen," Pauline replied, "I live less than a kilometre from you. It's not a problem for me to drive you to the practices and games. The school and homework issue is, of course, between you and your parents."

"Well, the other thing is ..." Quyen began.

"Anna?" Pauline guessed. She exited the Queensway and stopped at a red light.

Quyen nodded.

"Well, I don't know what the story is with Anna. She seems to be a complicated girl, not easy to get to know. She hasn't exactly warmed to *me* so far." Pauline turned onto Quyen's street.

Quyen took a deep breath and started to explain. "Anna bullied and harassed Ammi when they were both at Queen Victoria last year. It got so bad that Ammi ended up having to transfer to McClung. It didn't stop there. When the Queen Vic team came to our tournament in the spring, Anna started right where she'd left off. The whole thing shook Ammi up pretty badly."

Pauline pulled into Quyen's driveway. She put the car in neutral and faced Quyen, a grim expression on her face. "I'm sorry to hear that. No one should ever have to go through anything like that and I can't think of anyone less deserving of such treatment than Ammi." She paused briefly. "Now, I barely know Anna Archer, but I can tell you one thing for sure. This is a girl who has to have suffered in some way herself to have become so bitter by the age of thirteen. I'll bet you anything that if Anna's into hurting others, she must have some pretty major pain of her own."

"Hmm …" Quyen responded. "I don't know about that. But I *do* know that *I* wouldn't take anything from her."

"No, I don't think you would, Quyen," Pauline said with a smile. "So, does that mean you'll play?"

"I'll talk it over again with my parents, Pauline," Quyen answered, knowing that her father was not likely to have changed his mind since their earlier discussion. "I really can't promise anything. Thanks for the ride."

Quyen climbed out of the car and came around to the driver's side. The afternoon was warm and Pauline's window was rolled down.

"So you really think I'd be good for the team?" Quyen asked sincerely, bending down to Pauline's eye level.

"Not only do I think you'd be good for the team, Quyen," Pauline said, smiling. "I think the team would be good for you."

* * *

Quyen was pleased to see that her mother seemed to be feeling well that evening. Mrs. Ha rose after dinner to start putting away food, and Quyen was quick to point out that it was her turn to help clear the table and load the dishwasher. Mrs. Ha was humming an unrecognizable tune, which Quyen took to mean that her mother was in a better mood than she'd been in days.

"I got back my first math test today, Mother," Quyen said. "I received a mark of 97 per cent."

"That is a very good mark, Quyen. You must keep working hard."

Quyen bit her tongue. It was customary for her parents to expect academic excellence from their daughters. Both Quyen and Ming were in special classes for intellectually gifted students. Quyen knew her mother's prompting was out of sincere encouragement rather than reproval, but she wished that just once her parents would say "Well done!" when informed of a mark that most parents would celebrate.

"Actually, I misread a number on one of the problems. The way it was printed, I thought it was a six, but it was an eight," Quyen explained. "I pointed it out to Mrs. Moyles, but she just laughed and said it was the highest mark in the class, so I shouldn't be concerned."

Her mother nodded and Quyen decided to continue the conversation on another topic. "Mother," she said, "remember I mentioned that I wouldn't be playing on the volleyball team at school because I couldn't get to running practices?"

"What does running have to do with volleyball?" Mrs. Ha asked innocently.

"Yeah, exactly," Quyen mumbled under cover of the dishwasher's noisy hum. Then more loudly, "Oh, just some rule Ms. Bradford has. Anyway, I was wondering if you and Father would allow me to play on a basketball team outside of school time. It's called the Shooting Stars and they practise every Wednesday ..."

"What's this?" Mr. Ha said crossly, standing at the kitchen door. "I have already told you that there will be no special drives for sports. Next year you are in high school. Now you must concentrate on your studies."

Quyen faced her father. For the last while, he had seemed to be constantly short of patience with his daughters. Quyen felt her face flush, an unaccustomed sensation, and her hands clenched, a rare experience.

"Father," Quyen began evenly. Not once in her entire life had she ever talked back to either one of her parents. "Father, I respectfully request you to tell me how Ming and I can be more obedient daughters than we are, how we can make you smile again and not be angry with us, how we can do better in school than standing at the very top of our classes, how we can make you happier with us and make you love us again."

Quyen was shaking. She felt tears welling in her eyes, but she would not allow them to fall. Ming stood behind their father, wide-eyed in disbelief at Quyen's outpouring of what the two sisters had discussed privately in hushed whispers over the last several weeks.

Quyen turned at the sound of a muffled sob escaping from her mother and watched as Mrs. Ha ran from the kitchen, nudging her husband aside as she passed through the door on her way up the stairs to her room.

Quyen caught a look of deep concern on her father's face as his wife fled, before his features settled back into their usual stern expression.

Mr. Ha turned to his older daughter. Unexpectedly, his look gave way to one of sorrow. Quyen feared that her father would break down, and she didn't know if she could bear it. She knew she had been out of line — in her family it was unthinkable for Ming or her to ever talk back to their parents — and she marvelled once again at just how much her normal personality had been altered by the dramatic changes in her parents' behaviour throughout the summer and into the fall.

"Father, I ..." she began.

Mr. Ha held up a hand to quiet her. He seemed to have recovered his composure. "This basketball you want to play," he said softly. "You will tell me everything about it ..."

"But ..." Quyen interrupted, intending to withdraw her request to play.

"Tomorrow," her father said firmly, lowering his raised hand. "Now we will rest. Things will look brighter tomorrow." He turned slowly and walked with a heavy step past the stairway toward his office at the front of the house.

Quyen and Ming exchanged a look of shared helplessness.

5

An Unpleasant Introduction

Girls," Pauline began, "Coach Andrews and I would like you to welcome a new player to the team. This is Quyen Ha. Quyen is in grade eight at Nellie McClung Middle School — the same school I went to!" she finished proudly.

Quyen stepped towards the team and nodded her head briefly, a neutral expression on her face. The last impression she wanted to project was one of eagerness. What if nobody on the team wanted her around?

"I don't get it," a voice said casually from the back of the group seated on the gym floor.

Quyen cringed inwardly. Anna Archer. Quyen had expected no less; she figured Anna would show her true colours right away.

Well, Quyen thought, *I'm ready for you. I didn't go through hell with my parents to play on this team just so your snobbish attitude could make my life miserable, Miss Anna Archer. I am not Amelie.*

"What is it you don't get, Anna?" It was Coach Andrews who stepped in to respond.

"First of all, Quy-en," Anna said, pronouncing Quyen's name with an exaggerated accent, "didn't go through the tryout for this team. What about the fifteen girls who got cut? Shouldn't one of them get a chance at this opening?"

"Good question, Anna," Coach Andrews replied. "It shows your sense of fairness to wonder about those who were cut."

Quyen could not detect a trace of sarcasm in his response.

"However," the coach continued, "Quyen is a point guard. There wasn't a single athlete among those who tried out and were cut who was a potential point guard. Furthermore," he continued, fixing Anna with a pointed expression, "I have seen Quyen play and Pauline has coached her. I think, between us, we have enough basketball experience to be able to make an appropriate decision based on what we've seen. Did you have another point you wanted to make?"

Undaunted, Anna continued her assault. "*Quy-en* doesn't go to Ashwood. I thought you wanted to make this a combination school and club team."

"Hey, Anna, I don't go to Ashwood," piped up one of the seated players.

"Me either," added another.

"Yeah, well, you two are different," Anna said sullenly. "Mr. Andrews was your coach before this team was started."

"So?" the second girl retorted.

It struck Quyen that she might not be the only one irritated by Anna's attitude.

"Enough, girls," Coach Andrews interrupted, finally impatient with the quibbling. "We are lucky to have Quyen — that's pronounced 'Quinn' — joining us. You'll see that soon enough. Now, let's get going. The season opens in a few weeks and, judging from the game we played against the Badgers on Saturday, we've got a long way to go to meet the goals we've set for ourselves."

Quyen flashed a very small smile with only a hint of victory in it in Anna's direction as the unhappy girl got lithely to her feet, appearing intent on ignoring Quyen's existence.

This might actually be fun, Quyen told herself. Not only will I get to play basketball on one of the best teams in the region, I'll also be making Anna miserable — no less than she deserves for everything she put Amelie through. And the best part is that I won't have to do a darned thing other than show up.

* * *

Soon, the Shooting Stars were working up a sweat from a rigorous warm-up led by Pauline. They completed that portion of the practice with pro sprints, killer repetitions of short distances, complete with several changes of direction.

Like every other player, Quyen hated the tortuous speed drill, but she was fast and agile and never had to do the extra sets that were required of the girls who finished last.

"Man, are you ever fast!" said a teammate who came up behind Quyen at the drinking fountain as she refilled her water bottle. It was one of the girls who had spoken up about not being an Ashwood student.

"Thanks," Quyen said quietly. She hated compliments — she never knew what to say, and eventually settled on the simplest response possible.

"I'm Katie," the girl continued, taking her turn at the fountain. "I go to Broadbent. Welcome to the team."

Quyen studied the other girl as she filled her bottle. Katie was a couple centimetres taller than Quyen and several kilograms heavier. She was solid without being fat. Quyen remembered her from Saturday's game. Katie was a post player, the same position as Anna, but Quyen thought she had also played the power forward position once or twice in the game.

"I live near Broadbent," Quyen said as the two girls walked back to the gym.

"Yeah? Well, let me know if you ever need a ride to practice. Maybe our parents could carpool to the games!" Katie said enthusiastically.

"Sure," Quyen replied, sorry she had revealed where she lived. The conversation with Father was still fresh in her mind.

"Very well, Quyen," he'd said sternly, "if your coach will drive you back and forth *and* as long as you maintain excellent marks, you may try this Shooting Stars basketball team. Any problems," he had paused for effect, "and that's it. No more basketball. Understood?"

Quyen had nodded her understanding and thanked her father for giving her the opportunity to play.

Back in the gym, Coach Andrews began explaining the next activity, a simple passing drill in partners. Katie joined Quyen, and the two girls practised chest and bounce passes, two-handed overhead and baseball passes. Soon, they fell into an easy rhythm and Quyen turned up the speed of her passes a notch. She was pleasantly surprised to find that Katie had no trouble handling the heat.

During the next hour, Pauline and Coach Andrews led the players through a series of progressively more challenging drills, all of which Quyen executed with quiet, explosive perfection. She felt energized by the team and sensed that they felt energized by her. She hadn't imagined that making the transition to teammate with these girls would go so smoothly. Only Anna had steadfastly refused to acknowledge Quyen's existence, and had so far managed to avoid participating directly with Quyen in any drills.

"Okay, girls, take five minutes," Coach Andrews called out.

Quyen headed for her water bottle, which was at the end of one of the benches. She sensed someone approaching her from behind.

"I would suggest you don't do anything to make me look bad in the scrimmage," said Anna in a low voice.

Quyen turned around slowly. "Now why would I do that, Anna?" She paused, then looked Anna straight in the eye. "You're perfectly capable of doing that all by yourself." She picked up her bottle and brushed by Anna in the direction of the players' locker room.

* * *

"Okay, girls," Coach Andrews began when the team had all gathered back at the bench. "In this scrimmage, there's no dribbling ..."

Several girls moaned.

"With one exception," the coach continued. "If you receive a pass on the run as you're breaking to the basket, you can dribble in for a layup. Any other time, dribbling forces a turnover. On blue I want Quyen at one, Justice at two, Kalli at three, Alexia at four and ..."

Quyen noticed the hesitation.

"... and Katie, you play five on blue."

Quyen noticed that Anna's faced relaxed a little when she heard that she wouldn't be playing on the same side as Quyen.

Don't get too comfortable, Anna, Quyen thought to herself. *You're going to have to do your part to help this team get better. And you're going to have to do it by dealing with me.*

The two lines playing against each other as blue and red would have been well matched if Quyen hadn't been the blue team's point guard. She controlled the ball expertly and made passes that moved like they had a built-in radar system to the receiver's outstretched hands. Quyen set up plays that, for the most part, worked very well, considering she had never before played with these girls. Errors were made, but they were minimal, and the blue team gradually dominated the half-hour scrimmage, although no score was officially kept.

When Pauline finally blew the whistle to end the scrimmage, the weary players jogged two laps of the gym slowly to cool down, then spread out to stretch briefly before gathering up their belongings.

Quyen had observed Anna's growing frustration at having few opportunities to score. The red team had done poorly at getting the ball to her at the post. Katie, on the other hand, had led the blue team's scoring, playing the same position as Anna was playing for the red team. Quyen wondered briefly whether Anna would consider this making her look bad.

"Ready to go?" Pauline asked Quyen.

Quyen nodded and she and Pauline headed together towards the exit.

"Hey, Quyen!" It was Coach Andrews calling to her from the bench. "Great practice! We're really glad you came out!"

"Thanks, Coach," Quyen said. "See you next week."

The parking lot was dim, just two tired lamps throwing a weak light across the asphalt. Pauline unlocked the passenger door for Quyen and came around to the driver's side. "Way to go, Quyen. You were awesome," Pauline remarked as she climbed into the car and buckled her seatbelt.

"It was really fun, Pauline," Quyen replied quietly. "Most of the girls seem great!"

"They really are a good bunch," Pauline said, putting the car into gear. "You can't let one rotten apple spoil the barrel!"

I don't know about rotten apples, Quyen thought to herself, *but I know a rotten attitude when I see it.*

6

Just Hangin' Out

It was a Thursday afternoon, sunny and warmer than usual for early October. Quyen felt a little uncomfortable entering the McClung gym with Amelie for the Cougars' volleyball practice. It had been a few weeks since the big cross-country talk with Ms. Bradford. Quyen did, after all, have her as a gym teacher as well and they had enjoyed an excellent teacher-student relationship throughout Quyen's grade seven year. Although things had seemed a little strained right after the incident, Ms. Bradford had quickly returned to her usual friendly and casual manner. Quyen thought her teacher might have tried to bring up the subject, had even seemed prepared to apologize, but Quyen had deflected the discussion, still uncomfortable with her own handling of the situation.

Now she was going to be at a team practice, when she wasn't on the team — this would be a first.

"I told you Ms. Bradford said it would be absolutely okay for you to come watch the practice!" Amelie said. "I told her you were coming to my house for dinner."

"Aren't I?" Quyen asked seriously.

"You'd better be!" Amelie said, laughing.

"By the way, Ammi," Quyen said, "you haven't mentioned the math test. How'd it go?" Amelie struggled with math. Early in their friendship Quyen had started helping her with the subject and Amelie had improved to marks in the average range.

"Oh, yeah, I almost forgot," Amelie replied, a big grin wrinkling her freckled nose. "I got 78 per cent!"

"Awesome," Quyen said, delighted for her friend.

Quyen sat down at the end of the bench that was closest to the doors. She watched as the practice began with a warm-up. Ms. Bradford started a passing drill and, as the players got into the rhythm of the activity, she started to walk toward where Quyen was sitting. Quyen thought that maybe, after all, the time had come to bring things out in the open.

"So, Quyen, Pauline tells me you're playing with the Shooting Stars," Ms. Bradford said as she neared Quyen.

Quyen relaxed when she saw her teacher was smiling. "Yes," she replied, "it's been a couple of weeks now. I really like it."

Ms. Bradford sat down. "Betcha didn't know that I started that club."

Quyen was surprised and she shook her head to indicate that she hadn't known.

"Yep, it was five years ago when my daughter Jamie was in grade five. There weren't any girls' basketball programmes in the city so a friend — whose daughter was the same age as Jamie — and I decided to start one together. And that was the Shooting Stars!"

Quyen could hear the pride in her teacher's voice.

"Wow, that's pretty cool! How many players did you have the first year?"

"Sixteen," Ms. Bradford replied. "Sixteen little grade fives and sixes. They were so bad — we really had no idea what kind of a competitive league we were getting into!"

"Did the kids like it?" Quyen asked.

"They loved it! Those poor little girls would get beat, like 43–6, and they would be just as happy as clams. You could see their self-esteem develop right before your eyes." Ms. Bradford paused and smiled at Quyen. "Because they were part of a team!"

Quyen returned the smile. As Ms. Bradford rose to return to coaching her team, she turned back toward Quyen. "I'm glad you've joined the Stars, Quyen. They'll benefit from your leadership."

"Thanks, Ms. B." Quyen said, meeting her teacher's eye. "And thanks for starting the club. Your daughter was really lucky to have you for a mom."

"Someone should tell *her* that," Ms. Bradford laughed as she walked away.

* * *

"I can't believe Ms. Bradford ended the practice twenty minutes early," Amelie whispered to Quyen as they left the gym. "She *never* does that!"

"Well, don't complain about it! Now we can go to Ida's for something to drink before your mom picks us up."

"Sounds good. I'll tell Jill and Mei-lin," Amelie volunteered.

After changing, the four friends left the school and crossed the street to Ida's, a small family-run restaurant where the girls would occasionally get together after practice for a snack or a cold drink.

"So Quyen, tell us about your basketball team," Mei-lin said as the girls seated themselves at a booth in the cozy little café. "We didn't have a chance to talk at Vietnamese school on Saturday."

"Yeah, Quyen, tell us what's going on with the rich girls' team," Jill said, obviously in fun.

"Come on now, you guys, not every girl on that team has money. A couple girls who go to Ashwood are there on academic scholarships," Quyen replied. "Actually, except for one," she said, glancing at Amelie, "the girls are all pretty nice. I'm enjoying playing with the team."

"She's being modest again," Amelie said playfully. "Quyen is the star of the Stars. I heard Pauline say that to Ms. Bradford."

Quyen shot Amelie a warning glance. Her friend knew how much Quyen hated boasting.

"Oops! Sorry, Quinnie. Forgive me?" Amelie asked earnestly, her mop of brown curls bouncing as she nodded her head to get Quyen's approval.

"Let me think about it ... okay, you're forgiven," Quyen said sternly. It was impossible to remain annoyed with Amelie, Quyen reflected. She was just too ridiculously easy-going and way too much fun to be with. As different as they were, Quyen could hardly believe how close they'd become in the year they'd known each other. Although Quyen had many friends, Amelie was the only one who had succeeded in getting her to open up about herself. Quyen knew her friends regarded her as reserved and uncommonly private.

Ida came over to take the girls' order and, after they all asked for a soft drink or some juice, Quyen continued. "It's not the same, you know, as playing with you guys. When it's with your friends and for your school ..." Quyen paused, feeling a little uncomfortable. "Well, you know, it's just better."

Amelie came quickly to Quyen's assistance. "That's right, it's *cool* to play for your *school*, but you can be sure we'll all play together again."

All four girls nodded their agreement.

"What about Anna?" Amelie asked. "Has she made any trouble?"

"Actually, it's funny. Anna wasn't at the practice last night. The coaches said she was sick, but I wondered if she was going to leave the team because I've joined," Quyen said.

"Do you really think she might?" Jill asked, surprised.

"I don't know her well enough to guess one way or the other," Quyen replied, sipping the orange juice that had just arrived.

Amelie shook her head. "No way," she said seriously. "Anna Archer does not scare off."

What in the world, Quyen wondered, not for the first time, *ever happened to make that girl so spiteful?*

Quyen knew that she could outlast any prolonged mental assault from Anna, but she wasn't so sure she had the strength to endure much more sadness and secrecy at home. While the others chatted, Quyen sat quietly and reflected on the latest development. Earlier in the week, she had arrived home from school to find their family doctor just leaving. Despite the fact that Dr. Nguyen was a long-time family friend, Quyen could not help wondering if he had really been there for a friendly visit, as her mother had insisted, or if he'd been attending Mrs. Ha for medical reasons.

For Quyen and her sister, the mystery continued to grow, with no solutions in sight.

7

Figuring Things Out

On Saturday, Quyen and Ming walked home from Vietnamese school, discussing, as usual, their latest theories about what was going on with their parents. It was late October and the trees had given up most of their leaves. A few curled, brown ones clung tenaciously to the mostly bare limbs of the maples, the poplars, and the occasional oak that lined the streets of their old west-end Ottawa neighbourhood.

"They've both been pretty quiet this week, don't you think?" Ming asked her older sister.

"Um-hmm," Quyen answered, deep in thought. "It almost feels like what Ms. Bradford calls 'the calm before the storm.'"

"Yeah, I know what you mean. It's weird the way they just keep trying to act like everything's normal," Ming said.

"Well, I don't think they can keep this up. I mean, talk about *stress!*"

The sisters turned up the walkway to the front door of their colonial-style, two-storey brick house with white trim. The flower beds, tended so lovingly by Mrs. Ha throughout the warm summer months, had been dug up and turned over. They stood like freshly-dug graves, tucked up next to the front of the house and lining the walkway. Quyen had always found the sight of the empty, autumn garden beds inexplicably sad.

As usual, they entered the house quietly, but were surprised to hear no greeting from either parent. Then Quyen held a finger up to her lips, telling Ming to be quiet. From their father's office, she could hear the low voices of her parents.

Motioning her sister to follow, Quyen tiptoed down the hall and inched her way to the partly open door, signalling Ming to wait a few steps back. Quyen peeked into the room. Her father was on the phone speaking in Vietnamese and her mother was sitting on the couch behind her husband's chair. She was rocking herself and holding her head in her hands.

"What's going on?" Ming whispered.

"Shh!" Quyen hushed softly.

She couldn't hear her father clearly but caught a few words and then a question. Mr. Ha was asking something about how long it would be before they knew for certain.

Puzzled, then frightened, Quyen backed away and tiptoed with her sister to the front door. She opened it silently, then closed it with a bang.

"Father!" Quyen called out. "Mother, we're home!"

Quyen and Ming walked slowly down the same hallway where Quyen had, only moments before, been spying on their parents. She pushed open the door to her father's office and the girls entered. Mr. Ha was no longer on the phone and Mrs. Ha appeared composed. The parents and daughters stared at each other in a kind of bizarre standoff for a few seconds before Mrs. Ha smiled weakly and told the girls that lunch was almost ready.

* * *

The rest of the day was uneventful, but relaxing and enjoyable. Amelie and a friend of Ming's came over in the afternoon and the four girls played computer games and talked about school. The friends stayed for dinner and Mr. Ha drove them to a movie, where Ming and Quyen stuffed themselves with popcorn and laughed with their friends at the ridiculous antics of the characters in an outer-space adventure spoof. The heroes in the film were attacked by aliens that looked like giant, mutant bugs.

"I can't believe I paid to watch that!" Quyen said as they left the theatre.

"What a way to go, zapped by an overgrown mosquito!" Amelie said, rolling her eyes. "Oh, there's my dad's car!"

"Are you staying at your dad's tonight?" Quyen asked.

"Yeah, another Saturday night pretending that the broken-down sofa bed is comfortable," Amelie laughed. "Just be glad that, whatever else may be going on, at least your parents still live in the same house."

Quyen marvelled at Amelie's unfailing good nature. She knew that the separation of Amelie's parents was a source of pain for her friend. Yet Amelie always tried to make the best of her situation, and continued to believe that her mother and father would eventually reconcile.

Amelie's father dropped Quyen and Ming at home by nine-thirty. Their mother had gone to bed and Mr. Ha was reading in the living room. The sisters said good-night to their father and went upstairs to get ready for bed.

"Are you going to tell me now?" Ming asked as she pulled her comforter up under her chin.

"Tell you what?" Quyen said, innocently. She was also settling herself into bed, luxuriating in the feel of clean sheets on her bare legs.

"Very funny, Quyen Ha. You know darned well I've been waiting all day to find out what you heard when we were outside Father's office today. Now, don't tease me."

"Okay, Little Sister," Quyen began, using her pet name for Ming. She explained to Ming what she thought she had understood her father to say.

"'When will we know for certain?'" Ming asked, repeating what her sister had said. "Know *what* for certain?"

"Well, I guess it could be just about anything," Quyen replied. "But Mother was in on this conversation — I think she was crying — so I don't think it was about Father's business, unless there's some really serious problem with it."

"What kind of problem could there be with the pharmacy? Father just hired two new assistants to keep up with all the business!"

"You're right, Ming," Quyen said. "It's definitely not business. So what does that leave? Divorce? Illness?"

Quyen saw that her younger sister looked startled at that, as if she hadn't ever thought of it, as if the girls had not discussed the possibility of one of their parents having a health problem about a million times. The visit of Dr. Nguyen earlier in the week had seemed to lend further support to that theory.

"Not divorce. Why would he ask when they 'would know for certain?'" Ming wondered.

"No, not divorce. Mother and Father almost never even have disagreements, let alone arguments." Quyen thought some more. She regarded Ming. "It has to be something about their health, doesn't it? One of them must be ill and they're not telling us until they know for certain what the problem is or what's going to be done about it."

"Oh, Quinnie, it's scary to think that something might be wrong with either of them. We must ask. They *have* to tell us!"

"Calm down, Ming," Quyen soothed. "They're our parents. We have to trust that they know what they're doing and that they'll tell us what we need to know when we need to know it."

"But what if they don't? What if they just keep on hiding whatever it is and then it's too late? What if ..."

"Never mind the 'what ifs,' Ming," Quyen said firmly. "If you can't trust our parents, then you'll have to trust me. If things get much worse, I'll ask. I promise."

Ming sniffed and reluctantly agreed to remain patient. To Quyen's surprise, it was only a few minutes before she recognized by the gentle rhythm of her sister's breathing that Ming had drifted off to sleep.

I sure hope I'm not being totally naive, Quyen thought as she, too, edged closer to the oblivion of sleep. *If there's much more strain on my family, something — or somebody — is going to break down.*

8

Did I Hear Right?

The following Wednesday at practice, Quyen was only a little surprised to see that Anna had returned, looking as surly as ever. Mr. Andrews held a team meeting before the practice and Quyen observed that, as he gathered the players together, he was more serious than usual.

"The season begins in three weeks, girls," he began. "We'll be playing in the Western Division of the league."

"What about the Gloucester Badgers, Coach?" one of Quyen's teammates asked.

"The Badgers play in the Eastern Division," he replied. "Unless we arrange exhibition games or meet them in a tournament, we won't be playing the Badgers again until the championships in January."

"We have already entered a tournament we know they're playing in because their club is hosting it," Pauline said.

"In any case," Coach Andrews resumed, "I don't really want us to focus on the Badgers. We have several other challenging teams in our own division and, if we want a chance at Gloucester in the championships, we have to win our division first."

"In other words," Pauline interjected, "there's a lot of work to be done."

"Pauline's right," Coach Andrews said, "but even more important than working hard on the drills and scrimmages is working hard on being a team."

The coach paused for a moment and started making eye contact with each player individually. "Unless every one of you is committed to respecting, encouraging, and supporting each other, we might as well fold this team right now. Remember, there is no *I* in TEAM. You'll have to put any personal differences aside if this team is going to reach its potential."

Coach Andrews avoided singling out anyone, but Quyen knew that everyone was aware of the tension between her and Anna. Otherwise, all members of the team seemed to get along well and sincerely like one another.

"And another thing," Coach Andrews added. "We're going to need to practise twice a week from now on to be competitive. How's Sunday afternoon?"

None of the players had any objection, so the coaches advised the girls that they would now be practising two hours on Sunday afternoons as well as Wednesday evenings.

"And, of course," Pauline said, "once the season starts, most of our games will be Saturday mornings. You can count on playing about two Saturdays a month, come November."

Saturday mornings? Quyen had forgotten about that, and now wondered briefly how her parents would react to her missing so much Vietnamese school. *Fine by me*, she thought, *and they've already agreed to all this, so ...*

"Let's go!" Coach Andrews was calling. "Fifteen laps warm-up. Anna, how about if you lead the stretching?"

Quyen was surprised to see a smile on Anna's face in response. She practically glowed from the minor show of attention from Coach Andrews. After the girls had completed the jog, Quyen had to admit that Anna's stretching routine was considerably more thorough than that of most of the players, who usually just wanted to get through that part of the practice.

The coaches started with the familiar drills they had been doing for several weeks. Quyen usually paired with Katie and occasionally with one of the other girls for the drills that required partners. Since she had started practising with the Stars, Quyen was sure that their ability to pass and catch the ball had improved dramatically. Now and then, Coach Andrews put Quyen and Anna on the same line for scrimmages and Quyen deliberately created opportunities to give the ball to Anna in scoring position. The team had fallen into a relaxed pattern of high-fiving each other when a good play was made, but Quyen and Anna had yet to make any contact with each other since the brief conversation they'd had at Quyen's first practice four weeks earlier.

"Okay, girls, let's do some continuance," Pauline called out. "Passing only. Wing offensive players take over the defensive positions, unless you rebound the ball."

Continuance was a fast-paced full-court drill that the girls enjoyed. Done right, it was a good simulation of the game. The more aggressive a player was, the more opportunities she had to be in the middle of the action. The only other time the team had practised this drill, Anna had been away.

Quyen, Katie, and another teammate began passing the ball to one another as they moved downcourt to where two defensive players waited, one under the basket, the other at the top of the key.

"Ball, ball, ball!" shouted the player defending against Quyen, as she moved to establish position on her. Quyen had caught a pass at the three-point line, and three-point shooting was not her strength, although it was improving. Besides, Quyen understood that her job was to feed her teammates, so she protected the ball on her hip and pivoted until she saw Katie cutting across the bottom of the key toward her.

Quyen's defender was determined but not quick enough to recover when Quyen faked to pass right, then swiftly swung her right leg completely across her defender's body and fired the pass to Katie, who squared up and sunk her jump shot.

Katie followed her shot and grabbed the rebound.

"Outlet!" called Anna from the left-wing position. Katie passed her the ball and a third girl joined them from the right wing. The girls headed down to the far end of the gym. In the meantime, Quyen took up the low defensive position at her own end, under the basket, and waited for the action to return. She watched as Katie and Anna crashed the boards together at the other basket, but it was Anna who came down with the rebound and started the passing action back upcourt towards Quyen.

"Ball, I've got ball!" Quyen's defensive teammate cried, covering the girl in possession of the basketball at the top of the key.

Quyen stayed low in her stance, sliding back and forth across the key, trying to anticipate the direction in which the pass would be thrown. Suddenly Anna came towards her, but turned sharply at the key, her hands extended to receive the pass. As Quyen began to move to cover her, one of Anna's teammates stepped in her path, screening her from getting to Anna before she fired off a perfect turnaround jumper. As Quyen turned to get herself in position for the rebound, an elbow caught her smartly in the ribs.

"Out of my way, Chink," Anna whispered harshly as she whipped by Quyen to grab the ball as it fell through the net. Smoothly, she pivoted and fired the outlet pass to the next girl on the right wing and the three girls were away in the opposite direction, as Quyen stood still where she'd been hit, rubbing her side, her mouth open in disbelief.

In her entire life, Quyen had never been called a "Chink" or any other racist name that she could recall. "Maybe she said *Chick*," Quyen said to herself, shocked by the possibility that even Anna would stoop that low. "*Nobody* ever says *Chink!*"

Quyen recovered herself and moved to the end of one of the wing lines. The remainder of the drill was uneventful, but Quyen avoided being out in the action with Anna again. She was not afraid of Anna, but Quyen was terrified of what her own reaction might be if she and Anna got too close again, before Quyen had a chance to cool down. Her level of tension and strain was just too high to take a chance on losing her tightly reined self-control with Anna in a practice situation. If she was going to lose it, Quyen wanted to be sure she could also finish it.

9

Left Behind

On Friday morning, Pauline picked Quyen up at her home before anyone else in her family was awake. The McClung Cougar volleyball teams were leaving the schoolyard by chartered bus at seven o'clock to travel to Toronto for the provincial championships. Quyen was anxious to see her friends off, so Pauline had offered the early morning pickup when she'd driven Quyen home from practice on Wednesday.

"Still quiet, I see," Pauline said as she turned onto the ramp for the Queensway.

"What do you mean 'still?'" Quyen asked.

"Wednesday night after practice, it was like pulling teeth getting you to say a word. I think our only conversation was around arranging for this morning."

"Pauline, where do you get those crazy sayings? 'It's like pulling teeth' — what does that *mean?*" Quyen asked.

"I got them mainly from Ms. Bradford," Pauline replied, "I know *my* family never said anything like that — lots of other crazy things, maybe — but not like that." She paused and thought for a moment. "'It's like pulling teeth' means that something is really hard to do. You know, in the old days, I imagine pulling out people's rotten teeth with a pair of pliers was pretty difficult!"

"So you're saying you couldn't get me to talk the other night?"

"Something like that," Pauline answered, hesitation in her voice. She pulled over to the right-hand lane to take the Kent Street exit. "I know you tend to be quiet, anyway, Quyen. There's nothing wrong with that! But lately, it seems to be more a matter of being distracted, you know, preoccupied."

Quyen smiled to herself. It was only recently that she'd had to explain that word to Ming, and she'd been talking about their mother. "Thanks for your concern, Pauline. I'm all right. Really! I guess the thing with Ms. Bradford and not playing on school teams was a little more upsetting than I'd expected, but ..." her voice trailed off as Pauline pulled into the McClung staff parking lot.

"Well, let me know if there's anything I can do," Pauline said kindly. "I know you can put a lot of pressure on yourself."

"Thanks, Pauline," Quyen replied, getting out of the car. "For the ride, too."

"No problem."

Although it was early November, the temperature was still well above freezing during the day, and the McClung athletes who were gathered in the yard waiting for the bus to arrive were clad in sweatshirts or light jackets.

When she spotted Quyen approaching, Amelie raced to greet her. "Quinnie!" Amelie shouted. "I brought an extra-big bag that we can put you in so you can come along."

Quyen laughed. It was so like Amelie to think of how she could include others in her fun. Amelie was clearly in high spirits in anticipation of her trip, and Quyen suddenly had a serious pang of regret that she hadn't handled things differently so that she, too, could be part of the excitement.

"If I got in that bag, Ammi," Quyen said, "I'd miss my first league game with the Shooting Stars tomorrow."

"That's right — I almost forgot!" Amelie said, linking arms with her friend and walking back in the direction of her teammates. "How do you think it will be, playing in a real game with Anna?"

"Hard to say," Quyen replied, stopping at one of the benches just inside the mainly asphalted yard. "She's very competitive, so I'm sure the first thing on her mind will be winning the game — even if it means having to play and cooperate with me."

Quyen had not said a word to anyone, not even Amelie, about what she thought Anna had said to her during the practice. She hoped that she had misunderstood Anna. But something deep inside, some instinct, told her that she'd heard right. Quyen had still not decided what, if anything, she should do about it.

"Here," Quyen said, reaching into her backpack and pulling out a zippered plastic bag. "I made these last night for your trip."

"Oh, Quyen!" Amelie said with enthusiasm. "Your triple-C's! My favourite cookie in the universe! Thank you so much."

"Yep, the only thing in the universe I can make that's edible: chocolate cookies with two kinds of chocolate chips."

"So how are things, anyway, you know ... like, at home?" Amelie asked hesitantly.

"Hmm ... good question, Ammi. Only, I don't really know the answer," Quyen replied, then paused for a moment. "The fact is, Ming and I are almost positive now that something dreadful is wrong with Mother and they're keeping it from us. Yesterday afternoon when I got home from school, Mother was reading a letter. She didn't even notice that I'd come in!"

"Well, it must have been something interesting, or important."

"That's what I mean," Quyen continued. "The look on her face as she was reading ... I can hardly describe it — something between amazement and terror. As soon as she saw me, she folded the letter and put it away as if it was nothing at all."

"Did you ask her about it?"

"Yes. She basically told me it was nothing," Quyen said with resignation. "Ming and I are so frustrated with our parents, we don't know what to do anymore. It's a good thing I've got basketball and school to keep me sane ..."

"And me! Don't forget about me, Quyen," Amelie said. "Everything will be all right, and I'll always be there for you, to listen, or ... whatever! You're the last person who could ever go crazy, anyway, Quyen. You've got more self-control than anyone I know!"

"Hmm ... don't be so sure," Quyen replied doubtfully. "Hey, there's the bus. Let's go!"

Quyen and Amelie jogged over to join the rest of the team.

"What kind of secrets were you guys telling over there?" Jill asked, her eyes sparkling with excitement.

"Quyen was giving me her secret recipe for ..." Amelie brought the bag of cookies from behind her back. "... her triple-C's!"

"Sure she was," Mei-lin said, laughing. "You couldn't get that recipe out of her for a million dollars."

"You tell them, Mei-lin," Quyen agreed smugly. "I plan to make a fortune with that recipe some day."

"Okay, guys! Everyone line up," Ms. Bradford announced. "Leave your bags right here. The driver will load them. Just make sure you take whatever you'll need with you on the bus."

Quyen exchanged hugs with each of her friends in turn, Amelie last. "Have a great time, Ammi," she whispered. "Good luck."

"Thanks, Quyen. Same to you in your games tomorrow," Amelie replied. "And remember what you always tell me: worrying won't make anything better. I'm positive things will improve soon at home. I've just got a feeling that, whatever it is your parents are hiding, it won't be something awful. I really think they'd tell you, you know ... prepare you ... if it was bad."

"I hope you're right," Quyen said, smiling at her friend. She was consoled by the fact that Amelie was sensitive and perceptive. She seemed to have a knack for reading people and situations accurately.

Quyen gave a little wave. "Bye, guys." To herself, she added, in a whisper, "I'm counting on you being right, Ammi!"

10

For the First Time

The following morning, Quyen was up early again. Most Saturdays, she slept in until eight-fifteen and still managed to be at Vietnamese school by nine. But this morning, there would be no school. The season-opening basketball games for the Shooting Stars would be underway by eight-thirty and Quyen would be on the floor when the first ball was tossed up.

Quyen dressed and ate her breakfast quietly, hoping she could manage to get out of the house before her father got up. She had reminded him again the evening before that she would be playing basketball in the morning and he had acted like it was the first time he'd heard anything about it.

"What are you talking about?" Mr. Ha had demanded. "Of course you will go to Vietnamese school with your sister tomorrow."

"Father, I gave you a copy of my team's schedule, and I put tomorrow's games on the calendar in the kitchen three weeks ago," Quyen had explained calmly. "When I came home from practice last night, I mentioned it again. I'm sure you remember."

Mr. Ha had stroked his chin with his fingers, his eyes closed in concentration. Quyen hadn't known whether he was trying to recall what had been said or if he was just annoyed with her.

Finally, he spoke. "Ah, yes, I do remember now. And, if I am not mistaken, you have promised to make up any missed work."

"Yes, Ming will see that I am kept up-to-date. I will not fall behind, Father, I promise."

In the morning, Quyen was a little nervous that her father might start the whole thing over again. He no longer seemed able to retain information that was not important to him. Previously, before whatever was happening to distract him had begun, he never forgot a thing. No detail had been too insignificant for him to store and summon when required.

Quyen grabbed her gym bag and slipped out the front door. She did another mental check of its contents: uniform, shoes, ankle supports, water bottle, hair elastics. Everything was there — she was certain.

Following a quiet ride — Pauline seemed to be either very focussed on the morning ahead or not quite awake yet — Quyen and Pauline arrived at Ashwood more than a half-hour before game time. Coach Andrews was already in the gym, setting up the team benches and the scorer's table.

"Hi, Pauline, Quyen. Katie and a couple of the others are in the locker room," Coach Andrews said. Pointing to the electronic timer control box, he continued, "Pauline, could you give me a hand with this?"

Quyen entered the locker room to find Katie working on her hair. Katie's medium brown hair was too shaggy to be tamed by one hair elastic, so she had created two short pigtails high on either side of her head, while the rest of her hair hung loose. Quyen thought she looked ready for action.

"Hey, Quyen," Katie smiled her greeting. "How come you don't look like you just crawled out of bed? Every hair in place, no less ..."

"Well, everyone knows our new little point guard is simply perfect." Anna, emerging from one of the stalls, purred her sarcastic comment and even smiled thinly in a failed attempt at sincerity. Anna herself was the picture of perfection, her dark-brown hair pulled back into a sleek ponytail, her uniform exactly fitted to her tall, graceful body. She wore no jewelry or make-up but still managed to look like she'd just stepped out of the pages of a teen fashion magazine. *Elegant* and *sophisticated* were the words that came to Quyen's mind. *Perverse* was another.

"Why, thank you, Anna," Quyen said, also smiling, as she finished tucking her shirt into her shorts. "However, perfection is a state one aspires to, but never entirely attains, don't you agree?"

"Whatever," Anna muttered, her meagre attempt at civility totally abandoned. Grabbing her bag, she pushed through the door to the gym.

"How can you stand her?" Katie asked Quyen. "She's *so* rude!"

"I'm definitely not fond of her, Katie, but I'm not going to let her get to me," Quyen replied. "She's just looking to make me lose it, and I won't give her the satisfaction."

Quyen and Katie greeted some of their other teammates as the new arrivals entered the locker room and they exited. Out on the floor, the girls began shooting from various spots around the net. When the whole team arrived, they would begin their full warm-up. Anna and Quyen stayed well out of each other's way.

The first game was to be played against the Brockville Bobcats, and several girls in green and gold uniforms were warming up at the other end of the court. When the two-minute warning buzzer sounded, Coach Andrews summoned the Stars to the bench for one last pep talk and game instructions. Quyen, as expected, was to be the starting point guard and Anna, rather than Katie, would start at centre, also known as the post position.

"Okay, girls, this is what we've been preparing for," Pauline said in the huddle. "Let's show them what we've got."

"You know your jobs, ladies," Coach Andrews continued. "Just do them and the rest will fall into place. Anna, you remember the jump-ball play?"

Anna nodded silently.

"One! Two! Three!" Coach Andrews barked.

"*Stars!*" the huddled players shouted in unison.

The five starters hustled onto the floor and took their positions for the jump ball. Anna was slightly shorter than the Brockville centre, but her vertical jump and arm reach were several centimetres beyond her opponent's, negating the height difference. The ball was tapped into the hands of the Ottawa shooting guard. She fired a pass upcourt to Quyen, who was already within steps of the opponent's basket. One, two, and up she went, laying the ball gently against the backboard for the first two points of the game.

The game proceeded according to plan, with the Shooting Stars leading by a comfortable margin throughout the first half. The Bobcats were in disarray, turning over the ball frequently and struggling with their shooting. Anna was subdued, but energized enough to lead the Stars' scoring, thanks to Quyen's flawless passes to her as she stood in the low post, only a pivot step away from the basket.

"Great half, girls!" Pauline said, greeting the team enthusiastically as they came to the bench for halftime.

"Don't count your win until the game's over," Coach Andrews warned. "The worst thing we can do now is go back out there over-confident."

The coaches made a few adjustments in the team offense before sending them back out for the second half. Quyen and Anna continued to combine for the majority of points scored by the Stars, and the team ended up victorious by eighteen points over the Brockville team.

The Stars had a break while Brockville played against the Almonte Excels, who also defeated them. Quyen felt sorry for the Bobcats, this time beaten by twenty-seven points. The players wore weary looks of discouragement on their faces as they filed off the floor after the handshakes.

As expected, the Almonte team provided a greater challenge for Ottawa. The Excels were bigger, on average, than the Stars, and played with the confidence of a team that knows it has been well coached. After the Stars' starting lineup finished their shift five points behind the Almonte team, Anna sulked to the bench and announced that she wanted to play on a different line than Quyen.

"It just doesn't work with her and me," Anna said with a pout. "It's not the right chemistry."

"That'll be enough, Anna," Coach Andrews said calmly. "You can sit and think about that awhile." The coaches benched Anna for the remainder of the half. By that time, the Stars were down by twelve.

In the second half, Anna started, again with Quyen. Again, Quyen found it difficult to get the ball to Anna, mainly because of the excellence of the Almonte defense. Quyen observed Anna growing increasingly frustrated, but she managed to contain herself for the rest of the game. When it was all over the Shooting Stars had lost by seventeen points.

Coach Andrews could barely hide his disappointment at the loss. "Not because you got beat," he said, regarding his players earnestly. "But because you beat yourselves."

"Well, maybe if Quyen were from *here*, she'd know enough about basketball to make a decent pass!" Anna said fiercely.

This was met with stunned silence. Coach Andrews found his voice first. "Anna, you're suspended from the team for two weeks. After that you can return when you've apologized to Quyen and to this team for your behaviour."

"Well, that's not going to happen," Anna said coldly and then turned and stamped off to the locker room.

Quyen's teammates gathered around her and tried to offer comfort. But Quyen, who could not remember if she had ever felt so belittled, wanted nothing more than to get away from everyone.

Thankfully, Pauline saw Quyen's discomfort and suggested they leave immediately. In the car, Pauline said nothing for the first ten minutes, but Quyen knew that couldn't last.

"You've never had that happen before, have you?" Pauline finally said.

Quyen said nothing.

"Well, I can tell you, kid, that it has happened to me eighty-seven times in my life that I'm aware of. I know that because I remember every last incident," Pauline said with no show of emotion.

"No way," said Quyen.

"Yes," Pauline insisted. "And, furthermore, those incidents weren't just about where my family came from. No, they were comments about the colour of my skin, the size of my lips, my hair, my intelligence, my character!"

Quyen looked sideways at Pauline and saw a faint smile at the corner of her mouth. "Why are you smiling?" she asked. "There's nothing funny about that."

"It's funny, Quyen, if you get the last laugh," Pauline replied. "You know, every rotten, derogatory comment anyone ever made to me just made me more determined to make something of myself. You know, the old 'I'll show them' mentality?"

"There's no way it should be like that, though," Quyen said in frustration.

"I can't disagree with you there, Quyen," Pauline said as she pulled up in front of Quyen's house.

"Thanks for the ride," Quyen said, getting out of the car. "See you next week."

She walked a step away from the car, then turned back and approached the driver's side. When Pauline rolled down the window, Quyen lowered her head and said, "And thanks for the perspective."

When she entered the house, her father came up the hall from his office to greet her. "Quyen, what's happened to you? You are so pale!"

Quyen glanced in the hall mirror next to her and was shocked at her appearance. She was, indeed, ghostly pale and wide-eyed. She looked back at her father.

"Nothing, Father. I've simply exerted myself playing basketball," Quyen stated. "May I be excused to go shower?"

Mr. Ha regarded his daughter for a long moment. "Yes, a shower will refresh you," he said, nodding.

Quyen walked up the stairs to her room. *If my father will not share his troubles with me, then I will not share mine either,* Quyen said to herself. But the look of sadness on her father's face when she'd spoken was almost more than she could bear.

11

A Revelation

Fourth," Amelie moaned. "It's like a nothing finish. At least the boys got silver medals!"

Amelie and the volleyball teams had returned from their Toronto trip. They had been unsuccessful in their attempts to duplicate or improve upon their results from the previous year.

"Look," Quyen replied, "fourth out of forty-eight teams is pretty darned good! You did better than my basketball team did. We were only fifty per cent successful!" Quyen was relieved that her conversation with Amelie on Monday morning before school focussed on game results from the weekend. Her friend was so disappointed in the Cougars' showing in Toronto, she didn't even ask Quyen if there'd been any incidents with Anna. Quyen would tell Amelie about the insulting incident when she wasn't feeling quite so raw.

By Wednesday morning, Quyen found herself dreading the evening practice. She did not want her team's pity and intended to make that clear.

Surprisingly, the practice ended up being an excellent tonic for Quyen. It was a physically demanding workout and mentally challenging, with new plays being introduced. When it was over, Coach Andrews asked Quyen if she could stay for a few minutes. Pauline said she'd wait in the car.

Uh-oh, thought Quyen, *now what?*

When everyone had left the gym, Coach Andrews and Quyen were joined by an elegant looking woman — Quyen knew immediately it was Anna's mother. Sure enough, Anna followed behind, looking reluctant, at best.

"You're Quyen," Mrs. Archer said, smiling warmly and extending a graceful hand for Quyen to shake. "I'm Margaret Archer, Anna's mother."

Quyen nodded as she shook the woman's hand. She was not about to appear intimidated or to act grateful for the polite treatment.

Coach Andrews had pulled up a table and four chairs, one of which he held for Anna's mother. She smiled and thanked him as she sat, then indicated the additional chairs and waited until the other three had seated themselves.

"Thank you, Dave, for arranging this meeting," Mrs. Archer said to Coach Andrews. Turning to Quyen, she continued, "And thank you, Quyen, for being here. I understand that Anna has tried to make things uncomfortable for you."

Quyen met the woman's gaze. "Anna hasn't hidden her dislike of me," she said straightforwardly.

Anna's eyes stayed focussed on some invisible spot on the gym floor.

"Yes," Mrs. Archer said. "Well, if I could, I'd appreciate the opportunity to share some information with you in confidence. Anna and I have already been through all this. She's agreed to my telling you but she, um ..." she faltered.

"What my mother is trying to say is that I don't want anyone feeling sorry for me," Anna spoke up, her tone somewhere between defiance and entreaty.

"No offense, Anna," Quyen replied evenly, "but I don't think you need to worry about me feeling sorry for you."

"Why don't we just hear what Mrs. Archer has to say, Quyen," Coach Andrews interjected.

"Sorry," Quyen replied. "Please go on."

"We moved to Ottawa five years ago," Mrs. Archer began. "Anna's father was a senior attaché to the U.S. ambassador. Previously, we had lived in Mexico City for four years. I'm originally from Kingston, but Mr. Archer and I met at university in the States. In any case, we loved Ottawa ... at first. I was so happy to be back in Canada."

Mrs. Archer began to look uncomfortable. "Maybe I'd better go further back, back to my husband's youth," she said, then paused, seeming to collect her thoughts. "Jonas, my husband, had an older brother, Edward, whom he adored. Edward had been like a father to him, as their own father had died young."

Now it was Quyen's turn to feel uncomfortable. Did she really want to hear Anna's personal family history? She looked at her coach for support, but he seemed to be engrossed in Mrs. Archer's story.

"Anyway," Mrs. Archer began again, "to make a very long story short, when Jonas was thirteen, Edward was drafted and sent to Vietnam. Like so many other young men of the time, he didn't come back."

Quyen was certainly interested now. Where exactly was she going with this revelation?

"Jonas was devastated ... traumatized," Mrs. Archer continued. "To make matters worse, in her grief, his mother blamed the Vietnamese for her son's death. She became quite bitter and passed this racist attitude and opinion along to her impressionable younger son."

Quyen could still not quite comprehend how she was suppose to feel sympathy for these people whose decades-old ignorance now affected her.

"When Jonas and I met and married, I had no inkling of his deep-seated hatred for the people he held responsible for his brother's death," Mrs. Archer said. "Gradually, I came to realize how eaten up with anger he was inside and eventually, his emotions boiled over. By this time, we'd had Anna, and Jonas had worked his way up through the diplomatic service. When Anna was little, we lived in California and I began to notice that Jonas' bias included anyone of Asian heritage. But once we were posted to Mexico City, the strength of his prejudice seemed to dissipate. The Asian population in that city was small and it was a relief not to have to listen to his nonsense every time I turned around.

"I guess I thought the matter was closed," Mrs. Archer said, her voice a little shaky. "Then we were transferred to Ottawa."

Quyen knew where this was going now. Ottawa had an enormous Vietnamese community as well as Chinese, Cambodian, and other populations of Asian-Canadians and immigrants.

"The old issues resurfaced for Jonas. It seemed worse than ever." Mrs. Archer was now visibly distressed. "Apparently he was able to keep things together at work, but life at home became frightening. Jonas would have tirades, in which his anger and bitterness were expressed in uncontrollable rages. He never hurt us physically in any way, but, undoubtedly, these episodes had very adverse effects on Anna."

Quyen could no longer resist the urge to speak up. "You speak about Mr. Archer as if he's not here in Ottawa anymore. Did he leave?"

Mrs. Archer and Anna looked at each other. Anna's angry scowl had been replaced by a look of deep sorrow.

"A year and a half ago Jonas died — suddenly," Mrs. Archer explained, now in tears. "It has been very hard for Anna, for both of us. But until Mr. Andrews told me about what's been happening between Anna and you, Quyen, I really hadn't appreciated the depth of Anna's own anger."

"Thank you very much, Mrs. Archer," Coach Andrews said soothingly, "for your willingness to explain this to Quyen and myself. I think I can speak for both of us when I assure you that your privacy will be respected, right Quyen?"

"Of course," murmured Quyen who had never felt so awkward in her entire life. *Families can really make your life miserable*, she thought. *How could Anna's father have passed along such vile beliefs to his own daughter? Why hadn't Mrs. Archer been able to prevent it? And what*, she thought finally, *were the secrets her own family was keeping hidden?*

"Quyen," Mrs. Archer was saying, "Anna has just recently learned about all this herself. Changes in attitude take time. I hope you can be patient. Anna?"

Anna's blue eyes looked up at Quyen through wet lashes. Other than that, her expression was neutral. "Sorry, Quyen, for what I said."

Quyen wondered what was going through Anna's mind. The teary eyes seemed genuine enough, but why not? Anna's father had passed away less than two years ago, not long before Anna had begun her harassment campaign on Amelie. Had he taken his own life? Could Anna's grief and anger have been the force behind what she'd done to Amelie? Quyen knew that *she* would be devastated if she lost one of her parents. But she couldn't imagine taking it out on someone who had nothing to do with it!

As for this apology, Quyen thought that Anna had probably only agreed to it so that she could play with the team again. It was not at all evident that Anna meant it. Still, what could Quyen really do? She knew she would be expected to accept Anna's apology at face value.

"Okay," Quyen replied, still uncertain but deciding to give the benefit of the doubt. "Let's start over again. You know, for the sake of the team."

Both girls nodded their agreement, neither looking particularly happy.

12

The Best of Friends

On Saturday, Quyen went to Amelie's house for a sleepover. Since the Wednesday practice, and the extraordinary discussion that had followed it, Quyen had found herself even more introspective than usual. Ming had commented more than once in the past two days on how unusually quiet her sister was. But Quyen had kept her word and said nothing to anyone about Anna's situation.

The Shooting Stars had played a league game that afternoon against the Kanata Cavaliers, but Anna had not yet rejoined the team. Fortunately, the Kanata team was not very strong and the Stars were able to pull off a fairly easy win without Anna's contribution. Amelie had come to watch. Afterwards, Pauline had driven the two girls to Amelie's house in the midst of a mid-November snowstorm, but by evening, most of the snow had already melted.

"I can't get over how awesome your team is, Quyen," Amelie said, a string of pizza cheese hanging from her mouth. "The way you guys play seems so much more advanced than what we do on the school team."

The girls were in Amelie's family room, eating pizza and watching a video that was not as interesting to them as catching up on each other's news.

"Most of the girls have been playing with the Shooting Stars for two or three years, so they've had a lot of experience," Quyen replied. "Great coaching and lots of chances to play other good teams doesn't hurt either."

"Well, I don't know, but it's pretty impressive basketball!" Amelie said. "And *you* are the most impressive player."

"Okay, Ammi, let's not get carried away," Quyen said, trying to decide whether she should bring up the subject of Anna now. She wouldn't break her word, even to tell Amelie. Yet she knew that, of all people, Amelie deserved to know why Anna had such a hateful streak.

"So, why wasn't Anna at the game? You keep putting me off every time I bring up the subject," Amelie said.

"It's not that I'm putting you off, Ammi," Quyen replied cautiously. "But, you know, things aren't always what they seem."

"Where'd you get *that?* Is this another 'Bradfordism'?" Amelie laughed at her use of the term the girls had coined to describe the sayings favoured by their gym teacher.

"Fine," Quyen said crossly. "I'm just trying to say that sometimes people do and say things that they just can't help. Even *they* don't know why!"

"Okay, you've lost me. Are you talking about Anna now, or something else?" Amelie asked, genuinely perplexed.

"Oh, I don't *know* what I'm talking about. Anna, my parents, *everyone!*" Quyen knew her frustration was showing, but, for the first time in her life, she felt like everything going on around her was entirely out of her control. Here was her best, her dearest, friend in the whole world, trying to get some simple information from her, and she did not know how to respond. She put down her pizza and buried her face in her hands.

"Quyen! What is it? What's the matter?" Amelie asked, clearly alarmed by her friend's unexpected response. She moved over to put a comforting arm around Quyen's shoulder.

Quyen heaved a sigh. "I'm okay, Ammi. Really. I just lost it there for a minute."

"Hey, no problem. I'm your friend, Quyen, no matter what. You can tell me anything, but you don't *have* to tell me a thing."

Quyen decided. "Okay, let's start with Anna. First of all, she didn't play today because she was suspended from the team for two weeks."

"Oh my gosh!" Amelie gasped. "What for? What did she do now?"

"She said something about me after last Saturday's games. Coach Andrews told her she was suspended and that she would have to apologize to me and to the team before she could play again."

"Holy Smokes! What did she say to get herself in that much trouble?"

"To tell you the truth, Ammi, I'd rather not repeat it. Let's just say that it was kind of racist and definitely not complimentary."

"I guess not!" Amelie agreed. "So I take it she said whatever it was in front of everyone."

"Hm-hmm," Quyen nodded. "Anyway, she came with her mother after Wednesday night's practice and Mrs. Archer explained some family things that happened in the past that have obviously affected Anna in a pretty serious way."

"And you can't really tell me about these things, right?" Amelie guessed.

"I promised I wouldn't tell anyone," Quyen said.

Amelie seemed to consider that before replying. "That's why you're the best friend I've ever had, Quyen. Because I know that when you make a promise, you'll keep it."

The girls were quiet for a moment, each caught up in their own thoughts, then Amelie continued. "You know, Quyen, I'm just glad to finally know that there's a reason behind the way Anna treated me, that it wasn't because there was something wrong with *me*."

"Are you *kidding*?" Quyen replied. "Of course there's nothing wrong with you! No, Anna has actually had some pretty nasty experiences of her own and they were things that she had absolutely no control over. Anna and I will never be friends, but I feel like I understand her better now, and I even feel a little sorry for her. Of course, that's the last thing she wants."

"Right, I *hate* it when people feel sorry for me!" Amelie said. She reached over and turned the television off. They had not been paying attention to their movie for some time. "So ..." she continued casually, "what about you? Anything new with your parents? Have you figured out the big mystery yet?"

Quyen cleared her throat. She had some shocking news for Amelie. "Remember I told you that our family doctor was visiting the house a couple weeks ago?"

Amelie nodded. Her brown eyes were wide-open in anticipation.

"Well ..." Quyen began slowly. She felt almost embarrassed by the announcement she was about to make.

"Well, what?" Amelie said, starting to sound a little impatient.

"Well, our mother just told us today that Ming and I are going to have a little brother or sister next summer."

"What? Are you *kidding* me?" Amelie said, excitement evident in her voice. "That is *so* cool!"

"It is?" Quyen said. "I think my parents are a little old to be, you know ... making babies!"

"Gosh, Quyen, I'd *love* it if my parents were having a baby," Amelie replied enviously.

Quyen knew how much her parents' separation hurt Amelie. Of course she would think this was great news. "I guess it's okay, Ammi. I don't really mind the idea of a baby ..."

"But is that it?" Amelie asked uncertainly. She started counting on her fingers. "Eight, nine, ten. Is that what all the secrecy has been about? I thought things started getting weird at home at the end of the summer?"

"Exactly. My mom's expecting in July. So there's no way her being pregnant explains everything that's been going on with my parents."

"Did you ask her if there was anything else?" Amelie said.

"Sort of. You know how it is with my parents. Ming and I are expected to respect their privacy. It's not the same as it is with you and your mom and dad."

"Yeah," Amelie said. "I think I know what you're talking about. Like, you *never* argue with your parents!"

"It's just the way we were raised." Quyen shrugged. "Anyway, I did the math, too, and I definitely feel like there's something more. It's as if they think they're protecting us by not letting us know what else is going on."

Amelie nodded. "Before my parents split up, they tried awfully hard to hide their arguments. All it did was confuse Luke and me when they started to talk about separating. For a long time, we hadn't realized that their problems were all that serious."

"Exactly," Quyen agreed. "In a way, I feel angry that they don't trust Ming and me enough to tell us what's going on. Even though it's so obvious that something's wrong!"

"Right. It's like they think they're protecting you, when you're actually completely stressed out from all the hush-hush secrecy."

"Well, obviously you know exactly how I'm feeling," Quyen said.

"Even though *you* try to hide it, too, just like them," Amelie pointed out.

Quyen was a little surprised at the accuracy of her friend's observation. It had not occurred to her that she was covering up with her friends just as her parents were covering up with her.

13

Rematch

The next several weeks brought winter to the nation's capital. By the middle of December, ploughed snow was already piled to waist height along the sidewalks. At McClung, students received their first-term report cards. Quyen, keeping the promise she'd made to her father, brought home one of the best reports she had ever received. Mr. Ha was pleased, Quyen could tell, but he treated the accomplishment as if it was no less than he had expected.

"This is good, daughter, very good," he said, a serious expression creasing his forehead. "Do you suppose all this basketball you are playing is making you a better student?"

Quyen smiled, seeing her father's moustache twitching and his eyes sparkling. "Why, certainly it has, Father. All that exercise pumps more blood to the brain!"

"Hmm ..." Mr. Ha continued, still trying to appear grumpy, "shall we see if Ming can join?"

Ming had immediately jumped to her own defense. "Father, I had mostly A's on my report. There were only two B's!"

When she realized that she was being teased, Ming had joined her sister and father in a brief chuckle. There had been far too little laughter in their home for the past several months.

"There's Pauline. See you later," Quyen said, slipping into her boots and jacket and grabbing her gym bag from the bench by the front door.

It was the last Wednesday before the Christmas break and the Shooting Stars were off to play another exhibition match against the Gloucester Badgers. As she dashed out into the swirling snow, Quyen remembered how her teammates had groaned when Coach Andrews had suggested playing the Badgers again. She smiled to herself, thinking about how she had made eye contact with Anna, who had nodded slightly, and how she'd then spoken up in favour of the rematch.

"Easy for you," Katie had laughed. "*You* didn't play them the last time."

Quyen climbed into Pauline's car and brushed the giant snowflakes off her bangs.

"Do you think this snow is a bad omen for tonight's game?" Pauline asked with a grin.

"I'm not superstitious," Quyen replied and paused, "except about the number thirteen, and black cats, and broken mirrors, and ..."

"Okay, okay, I get the picture!" Pauline protested. "So, are you up for this game?"

"Definitely," Quyen said with a firm nod of her head. "I know the Stars have improved since the last time they played them, but I imagine the Badgers have gotten better, too."

"No doubt. They're undefeated in the Eastern Division," Pauline replied. "But even with our two losses, we're still in first place in the Western Division and, if we don't do anything really dumb in the meantime, it's likely that the regional championship will be between the Stars and the Badgers."

"So, I guess it's a good thing we play them in this exhibition game," said Quyen. "We'll have a chance to see what we're up against. Hopefully, we'll have enough time left in the season to improve where we need to."

"Sounds like a plan," Pauline agreed. She pulled into the parking lot of a relatively new suburban high school.

"What a beautiful school!" Quyen remarked as they entered the rotunda-like lobby.

"Sure makes our Centretown schools look dingy, doesn't it?" Pauline replied.

Quyen changed quickly and joined her teammates for the warm-up. Coach Andrews had asked them to try to resist looking over at the Badgers as they warmed up at their own end. "It makes them think you're intimidated by them," he said. "That's the last thing we want them to think."

Quyen's mind wandered a little as she went through the routine pre-game drills automatically. Watching Anna shoot in the line ahead of her, Quyen thought about the progress that had been made in their relationship since the apology. They had definitely not become friends, but play between them had improved remarkably and, in a game the previous week, Anna had actually given Quyen a high-five after Quyen had sunk a much-needed free throw towards the end of the game. It was the first time the two had made any physical contact whatsoever, despite the many hugs and handshakes that passed regularly between other members of the team. Working things out with Anna had taken all the patience Quyen could muster, something she'd always thought she had plenty of before the turmoil of the last few months.

"We've got a game plan," Coach Andrews said when the team gathered at the bench. "Let's try to stick to it."

"Make sure you warn each other about screens," Pauline reminded them. "Lots of talk out there. If you play with confidence, they'll think twice about taking you for granted."

The team gave their cheer and the starters ran onto the court. The Stars got off to a good start by scoring off the jump-ball play. The coach of the Badgers, known for being loud and often obnoxious, was on his feet, yelling non-stop instructions to his players.

The Stars played tough defense and the Badgers failed to score on their first possession. Anna rebounded the missed shot and fired the outlet pass to Quyen, who saw one of her teammates already driving towards the hoop. Quyen took two dribbles, then drilled the ball upcourt into the outstretched hands of the breaking Star, who easily made the uncontested layup. The Badgers had failed to hustle back on defense. Their furious coach called a time out.

"That was an outstanding two minutes of play," Coach Andrews said, grinning from ear to ear. "No matter what else happens, those are the four best points we've ever scored!"

"Be ready for them to adjust to the fast break, girls," Pauline added. "Mix it up, Quyen. Keep them guessing."

The Badgers did adjust successfully to the fast break but, as Pauline suggested, Quyen made sure to insert unexpected twists on the offense every time the Stars had possession. Nevertheless, the Badgers evened the score quickly and the teams traded two-point leads for the first half. When the buzzer went, the Stars led by a basket and the girls could not help chuckling at the panic-stricken voice of the Gloucester coach as he led his team into the hallway for the break.

The Badgers played their starting five for the entire second half, while the Stars' coaches continued to alternate the starters with the bench players.

"You never know who might have the game of her life on any given day," Coach Andrews explained with no apology for his decision. "Every player has to feel that her contribution is important in every game — because it is."

Unfortunately for the Ottawa team, the Gloucester starting five were in excellent condition and showed very little sign of fatigue as they gradually pulled away from the Stars over the course of the half. The game ended with the Badgers ahead by eight. Coach Andrews and Pauline were delighted with the way the team had played and claimed to be not the least bit disappointed in the outcome. The Gloucester coach, on the other hand, was still yelling at his team as they left the gym after the handshakes.

"What a difference it makes playing them with you on the team," Katie said to Quyen as the girls headed to their locker room.

"Thanks, Katie, but I think everyone on the team has come a long way since I saw you guys play each other back in September," Quyen replied.

"She's right," said a voice from behind. Holding the door open, Quyen turned her head and looked at Anna. Anna looked at Quyen. There was an awkward pause. "Yeah," Anna continued, no real expression on her face that Quyen could read. "The team is definitely better with you playing the point-guard position."

"Hey, Anna!" someone called from inside the locker room. "Eighteen points. Way to go!"

Anna stepped by Quyen and Katie through the door they were still holding open.

* * *

Pauline got Quyen home by nine o'clock. The following day at McClung, all grade eight students would be participating in a stock-market simulation for the entire day and Quyen was looking forward to the activity. She and Amelie and Jill had formed a company called JQA Consulting, and Quyen was responsible for bringing in some of the office paraphernalia they would need to create a realistic setting for their company.

"Mother?" Quyen called as she entered the house. Mrs. Ha was going to put together business attire for Quyen to wear the next day.

"Your mother has gone to bed," Mr. Ha said, coming to the door where Quyen was shaking the snow from her jacket.

"But ..." Quyen started to explain.

"She was feeling poorly, but she did ask me to see that you got this," Mr. Ha explained, extending a bag to Quyen.

Quyen regarded her father before reaching out to take the bag from him. Whether it was the exhaustion of the game, the anticipation of the following day's activity, or the disappointment of not being able to prepare with the help of her mother, Quyen was no longer able to contain her anxiety.

"Father, please tell me what is wrong," she implored him. "For weeks — no, months — even before the, um, the pregnancy, Mother has not been herself. Nor have you. She is always tired, or unwell, or distressed. Ming and I are very worried. Is there something wrong with Mother? Please ..." She trailed off, exhausted by the effort it took to ask the questions that had been in her heart for so long.

Mr. Ha was quiet for several moments, then spoke in a gentle voice that took Quyen by surprise. "My daughter, you must trust me when I say that you need not be worried. Your mother and I recognize that we have caused you and your sister to suffer these past several months. Please, be patient for a little while longer and everything will be revealed."

"But ..." Quyen could not help herself.

"A little while longer," Mr. Ha repeated.

"Yes, Father," Quyen finally said, feeling suddenly very tired and defeated. She wasn't sure how long "a little while" was, and she wasn't at all sure she could last even another minute without some answers.

But what can I do? Quyen asked herself. Remembering Pauline's odd saying, she thought, *Getting information from my parents is* exactly *like pulling teeth!*

14

A Holiday to Remember

At last the holidays arrived and Quyen, feeling physically and emotionally exhausted, was grateful for the chance to sleep in every day for two weeks. Plans had been made to go skiing with Amelie and Jill between Christmas and the New Year, but for now Quyen intended to enjoy the rest: no school, no homework, no basketball, no pressure.

The stock-market activity had been even more fun than Quyen had anticipated, and JQA Consulting had finished fifth out of the fifty-two companies formed by McClung's grade eight students. On Friday, the last day of school, there was a dance in the afternoon. Quyen lay in bed the following morning and reviewed the event. Dances were peculiar, Quyen decided. Everyone got all excited about them in the week or so leading up to the event. Then everyone ended up disappointed because the dance never lived up to the anticipation.

Daphne Jones, who had been Quyen's best friend before Amelie and was still a close friend, had been sent home from the dance and suspended from school for the first week in January. A teacher had caught her showing off a small bottle of vodka to some other girls in the change room. Daphne hadn't actually tried any of it, and Quyen was sure her friend was just looking for attention. The daughter of a single father who happened to be a cabinet minister, Daphne was often in the care of a housekeeper while her father travelled. Like Quyen, Daphne was not playing school sports this year and it seemed she was starting to get into other mischief.

"Did you hear about Daph?" Amelie had asked Quyen, following a slow dance. Pretty, athletic, popular, and just a little mysterious, Quyen was the most sought-after partner for slow dances by the McClung boys. Amelie, on the other hand, invariably took the opportunity to escape to the canteen with Mei-lin when the music slowed down.

"What happened?" Quyen was curious about her friend.

Amelie had shared the information she had, and Quyen had found the story of Daphne's misadventure depressing.

Now, lying in bed on a Saturday morning in late December, she remembered the stress test Ms. Bradford had given in health class back at the beginning of September. It was a questionnaire that assessed various life events and generated an index according to how many stressful situations a person was experiencing.

"Let's see," Quyen said to herself. She started to count on her fingers. "When I took that test, things were not going that crazy at home, I was looking forward to playing on the volleyball team with my friends, Anna Archer was not in my life at all, I didn't even know who the Gloucester Badgers were, and none of my friends carried vodka in their backpacks." She laughed. *How to go from zero to a hundred on the stress test in less than four months* … she thought.

"What's so funny?" Ming asked, sitting up in her bed.

"Funny? Nothing's funny, just messed up," Quyen replied wryly.

"Oh, come on now," Ming cajoled, climbing out of her bed and bouncing at the foot of Quyen's. "It's the first day of a two-week break from school and no Vietnamese school either! What's messed up about that?"

Quyen regarded her sister fondly and gave in. "You're right, Ming, I'm in need of an attitude adjustment, as Ms. Bradford would say. What do you feel like doing?"

"Eating breakfast!" Ming replied enthusiastically.

Quyen stepped into her slippers and pulled on her robe. "Let's go."

The phone rang as the girls descended the stairs. At the bottom of the staircase, Quyen started towards the kitchen, but slowed when she heard her father speaking excitedly in Vietnamese from his office. Then she heard her mother's voice, equally excited, interspersed with that of her father's. Suddenly, their voices dropped. Quyen and Ming looked at each other in confusion, then carried on into the kitchen.

"Daughters," Mr. Ha said, entering the kitchen with his wife a few minutes later, as Quyen and Ming were preparing bowls of cereal, "we have some news for you."

Quyen looked first at her mother who appeared to have been crying yet again. But this time her face was not sorrowful, it was alight with joy.

"Yes, Father," Quyen replied, a little warily. She could hardly believe that she and Ming might actually find out what mystery their parents had been guarding.

Quyen and Ming, their cereal forgotten on the counter, sat down at the kitchen table. Mr. and Mrs. Ha joined them.

"I am going to tell you a story," Mr. Ha began. "A true story, but a difficult story for the ears of ones so young."

Quyen and Ming looked at one another, then nodded their heads silently in unison.

"Very well," their father continued. "Many years ago, your mother and your father were in a refugee camp in Vietnam, hoping to be evacuated eventually. The war was coming to an end but there was still much horror, many bombings, many deaths."

Quyen knew that her parents had been evacuated from Vietnam at the end of the war. She had not been given details and would never have dared to ask. Questions relating to her parents' private matters had never been encouraged. She had simply assumed that their escape to Canada had gone according to some kind of plan and had been successful.

"In that camp with us was your mother's older sister and her year-old baby daughter," Mr. Ha said. Quyen thought she detected a slight catch in her father's voice.

Now this was information Quyen had not known. As far as she was aware, many of her parents' immediate family members had either died in the war or been scattered, their whereabouts unknown. Only her father's father had eventually come to Canada, where he had settled in Montreal and remarried.

"One day, unexpectedly, there was a raid on the camp. Fighter planes flew over, shooting at everything that moved. Your mother's sister and her child were separated from us. We tried and tried to find them. We called and called, but there was so much noise: the screams of the frightened and the wounded, the shouting of officials, the shooting from the planes, the confusion ..."

Quyen could see how painful the recollection of this story was for her father. She wanted to tell him that it was okay, that he didn't have to go through it all over again. But she recognized that there was something he needed his daughters to know and that he would continue his tale, even if it had to be through tears.

Mrs. Ha rested a hand gently on her husband's arm. Mr. Ha inhaled deeply and carried on. "Before we knew what was happening, your mother and I were being loaded like cattle into a truck that had been hidden under camouflage cover. We tried to explain that we must return to the camp for Lien and her daughter, Phuong, but we were physically detained in the truck despite our pleas."

Tears fell freely now from the eyes of both Quyen's mother and father as they remembered the torment of being forced to abandon Mrs. Ha's sister and her infant daughter. Mr. Ha brushed the tears roughly from his cheeks as he spoke. His wife sat motionless, her eyes focussed somewhere in the past.

Quyen got up from the table and put on water for tea. She needed to move, to reassure herself that she was here, in her comfortable home in Ottawa, in Canada, that her family was with her, safe and sound and free from the terror her father was describing.

"But, Father, there was nothing you could do!" Quyen offered, sitting back down, and feeling helpless herself.

"But one always wonders ..." Mr. Ha said wistfully.

"No, Dinh, our daughter is right," Mrs. Ha insisted. "I remember very well. There was nothing, nothing we could have done."

Mr. Ha considered this. "Perhaps. In any case, from the camp we were transported from one place to another before we were finally flown to Canada as refugees. At every stop along the way, we begged for information about the fate of your aunt and cousin, but we were unable to learn anything."

"Once we settled in Canada," Mrs. Ha continued, relieving her husband, for a moment, of the burden of his story, "we continued to make enquiries about Lien and Phuong, intending to never rest until we could learn what had become of them."

"Years went by," Mr. Ha said. "We made a new life in Canada. We had two beautiful daughters. Finally, this past summer it was confirmed that Lien had died in the camp the day of the raid, the day of our evacuation."

"Oh, Mother, how awful for you!" Ming cried. "No wonder you have been so sad."

"What about the baby?" Quyen asked quietly, rising to bring the teapot and cups to the table.

"We were not able to find out anything about the child," Mrs. Ha replied, simply.

Quyen saw her father's eyes fill again and realized as she looked at him that many of the lines on his face had been etched by the sorrow of this story. Knowing her father, she thought he must have felt that, as the man of the family, he should have been able to save everyone.

"Until now," Mr. Ha said softly.

"What's that?" Quyen asked, unsure as to whether she had heard her father correctly.

"For the last several months," Mr. Ha said, "we have been pursuing the possibility that Phuong is alive in Vietnam."

Both Quyen and Ming sat absolutely still, stunned at this news. Was it really possible, Quyen wondered. Do we have a cousin on the other side of the world? Our mother's sister's child?

"It is this investigation, my daughters, that has had your mother, and myself as well, in such a state of turmoil. You must understand that negotiating this investigation has been very difficult indeed. We did not feel it was appropriate to give you this information until we knew something definite."

"And now you do?" Quyen asked.

"It appears that the chances are good that Phuong is very much alive, a young woman now of twenty-six. Your mother will be travelling to Vietnam as soon as it can be arranged, to confirm her identity."

"How will you do this?" Quyen asked wondrously.

"The baby had an identification bracelet. Apparently this young woman is in possession of that bracelet," Mrs. Ha explained. "But a bracelet will not be necessary. I will know if it is Phuong when I look into her face."

The four members of the Ha family sat quietly, each with their own thoughts about the amazing story that had just been shared.

There's something else, Quyen thought, unable to pinpoint the source of her sudden puzzlement. But she knew with certainty that this was not the whole story, that there was yet more to be revealed.

15

Apologies and Appreciation

The Christmas holiday went by too quickly. Much of the tension at home was reduced once Quyen's parents revealed the secret they had been guarding for so long. Quyen was able to take it easy and enjoy her family and friends. She skied twice, went to see three movies, and read two books. Most of all, she felt relaxed for the first time in months.

Still, Quyen could not shake her sense that she and her sister had not been told everything. Where, for example, had her aunt's husband been while they were in the camp? There had been no mention of the child's father. Were they divorced? Or was there no husband? Perhaps this was a matter that was too shameful for her parents to tell Quyen and Ming. Quyen simply couldn't ask. She'd learned that information would be provided when her parents were ready. As a respectful and obedient daughter, Quyen knew she must accept that.

The day before Quyen was to return to school, her mother boarded a plane for Vietnam. The farewells were tearful because no one was sure when Mrs. Ha would return to her family. Everything depended on how quickly she could get the information she was seeking. The reunification of families could be quite time consuming. No one wanted any mistakes.

Now the hustle and bustle of the holiday season would give itself over to the hustle and muscle of school and basketball. Quyen didn't really mind going back. She missed seeing her friends every day, and she was beginning to look forward to playing again with the Shooting Stars as the team made its way towards the regional championships at the end of January.

Quyen had almost forgotten that McClung would be hosting its annual volleyball tournament for girls during the first week back, starting on the Wednesday afternoon.

"Promise you'll come every day of the tournament," Amelie pleaded on Monday when the two friends met for lunch.

"I don't have much choice, do I?" Quyen replied. "Ms. Bradford asked me this morning if I would organize the scorers."

"Perfect!" Amelie chirped. "Then you have to be there."

"Why wouldn't I?"

"Oh, I don't know," Amelie said cautiously. "I thought maybe you wouldn't want to hang around if you weren't playing."

"Well, of course I'd rather be playing, but, hey, that doesn't mean I can't have fun hanging out and watching you and Jill and Mei. Your pool is Thursday, right?"

"Yep. We play Broadbent, Hopevale, and one of the Scarborough teams — Bliss Carman, I think," said Amelie.

"Ooh, they're usually pretty strong, aren't they?"

"Hm-hmm," Amelie replied. "They won the silver medals at the provincials. Ms. Bradford figures that, even if they beat us in the pool, which they won't of course, it would put us in different brackets for the playoffs. That way, we won't have to face them again until the semi-finals if both teams advance that far."

"Ms. Bradford sure likes to think ahead," Quyen remarked.

"So did you tell her you'd look after the scorers?"

"Yes," Quyen replied. "But I told her I'd have to leave early on Wednesday for my practice, and I've got games Saturday morning."

"That's right!" said Amelie. "I could come watch if it's okay with you. The double-A playoffs don't start until the middle of the afternoon." Amelie paused for a moment. "You know, Quyen, I really think Ms. Bradford is hoping you'll play basketball with the Cougars when our season starts."

"We'll see," Quyen responded. She had wondered about that. Ms. Bradford and Quyen had never again discussed the disagreement they had had about cross-country training and playing on school teams. In fact, in many ways, they had carried on as if the falling-out had never occurred. Quyen had found it awkward at first — her entire grade seven year had been consumed with playing on every school team. She knew that Ms. Bradford had valued her contributions and Quyen had liked and respected her coach in return.

* * *

On Thursday, Quyen headed for the gym as soon as the bell rang. She went to work putting the scoring tables in order in both gyms, then helped the Cougars set up the nets and put out practice balls. The gyms started to fill quickly, not only with McClung fans, but with the visiting teams and their entourages of parents, family, and friends. The McClung Invitational was the largest elementary volleyball tournament in the province, attracting more than fifty teams from all over eastern Ontario and from as far away as Windsor, North Bay, and even Joliette, Quebec.

"Are you nervous?" Quyen asked Amelie when they'd finished all the preparations and the first matches were underway in both gyms.

"Well," Amelie said, "let's put it this way: I'm not as cool under pressure as you are, but I'm trying to stay calm and focussed. I know we've improved a lot since the provincials."

"I'd say so," Quyen agreed. "Oh, I think Ms. Bradford is getting the team together. Good luck!"

"Thanks, Quinnie. You have no idea how glad I am you're here to watch. My parents can't get here until the last game. It helps having someone cheering you on!"

Amelie skipped off to join her team for the pre-game meeting and Quyen settled herself on a bench to watch the end of the first match, in which Bliss Carman was pulverizing Hopevale, one of McClung's local rivals. Quyen thought about her friend Daphne, wishing she were here to watch the games with her, remembering a conversation they'd had on the phone two evenings before.

"What can I say? It was a stupid thing to do," Daphne had acknowledged about having brought alcohol into the school at the Christmas dance. Daphne had just returned from two weeks of skiing in Aspen with her father, but she sounded a little down. Quyen could relate.

"Hey, go easy on yourself, Daph," Quyen had advised. "We all make mistakes."

"You don't," Daphne had said.

Quyen was surprised by how her friends saw her as always cool, calm, and collected when, in reality, she had been such a wreck throughout the fall. *As for mistakes*, she thought, *what do you call being so stubborn that you — how would Ms. Bradford put it? — you cut off your nose to spite your face?* That's what she'd done in the fall when she'd refused to play on the volleyball team.

Lost in thought, Quyen did not notice Ms. Bradford's approach.

"Mind if I sit down for a minute?" her teacher asked.

Quyen smiled and moved down to make room at the end of the bench.

"Quyen, I've been meaning to talk to you for some time now," Ms. Bradford began.

What now? thought Quyen, noticing that her teacher seemed a little uncomfortable. "Sure, Ms. B.," she replied.

"Well, first of all, I want to thank you for all your help with the tournament. It's really appreciated."

"No problem. It's fun," Quyen said.

"Quyen, I ... I wanted to apologize to you for the misunderstanding about cross-country back in September," Ms. Bradford said. "Someone — it doesn't matter who — told me that you had only meant to ask if you could train at lunch instead of the morning. I was ... I was impatient and didn't hear you out. I don't remember anymore what my problem was that morning, but I was completely unfair to you."

Quyen was taken aback. Rarely, if ever, had an adult apologized to her. After a moment's thought, she replied. "Ms. Bradford, I think I also overreacted. I lost my temper and spoke without considering the consequences, so it's my fault, too. I apologize as well."

"That may be true, Quyen, but I have to tell you that it breaks my heart to see you sitting on the sidelines," Ms. Bradford said, "and I feel responsible."

Quyen reflected once again before responding. "I'm sure I would have enjoyed playing." She paused for a moment, then smiled, imagining her father's serious face. "When he wants us to look at the positive side of something, my father will sometimes says to Ming or me ..." Quyen made her face as stern as she could, "'Daughter, there is opportunity to be found in even the most unfortunate situation.'" She smiled again and shrugged. "If I had joined the volleyball team, I wouldn't have had the opportunity to play with the Shooting Stars."

"And you're enjoying it?" Ms. Bradford asked.

"Very much," Quyen replied, nodding thoughtfully. "So, thank you for the apology, Ms. Bradford, but, most of all, thank you for the opportunity."

Ms. Bradford stood, smiling broadly. "You're very welcome, Quyen. I hope you'll consider playing with the Cougars when basketball starts here."

The Cougars, dressed in their blue and gold uniforms, were starting to warm up as Ms. Bradford headed to the sideline. In red, their opponents, the Broadbent Bears, appeared to be considerably stronger than the Hopevale team that had just lost to Bliss Carman.

Quyen observed Ms. Bradford chatting amiably with the Broadbent coach. The rumour from the Cougars was that he and Ms. Bradford were "going out." Quyen smiled at the thought. It was kind of nice to think that older people could enjoy romance, although most of Quyen's friends found the idea gross.

In any case, Quyen could see no evidence of Ms. Bradford giving the Broadbent team the slightest advantage, as the Cougars beat the Bears in straight sets. Quyen chuckled. She knew from experience that Ms. Bradford liked to win and she encouraged a healthy competitive spirit in the players she coached. Amelie was beaming as she, Jill, and Mei-lin joined Quyen after shaking their opponents' hands.

"You guys were awesome!" Quyen said enthusiastically. "Way to go!"

"Thanks, Quyen," Jill replied. "But there were a few times out there when I especially missed playing with you."

No matter how well she or her team played, Jill always lacked confidence. She was the one who especially benefitted from Quyen's leadership when they played together and who missed her most — even more than Amelie — when Quyen was not part of the team.

"Hey, Jilly, that team didn't have a chance against your spikes," Quyen said. "You were really getting on top of the ball!"

Jill beamed. "Thanks, Quyen. Oops, I've got to run. Can you believe Mrs. Moyles is giving us a science test tomorrow? I swore to my mom I'd study between games. See ya later."

"Me, too," Mei-lin said. "Wait up, Jill."

"Congratulations, Ammi," Quyen said as the girls headed for the canteen. "You are the perfect captain out there. You can see everyone looking to you for team spirit."

Amelie smiled in response. They reached the front of the line and bought sandwiches and drinks, then found a relatively clean table in the corner away from the blaring television. Several kids were gathered around it watching a Toronto Raptors game.

"I've been meaning to ask you if you've heard anything from your mother," Amelie said after they'd settled at the table. Amelie was the only friend Quyen had confided in about the search for her cousin.

"She's phoned a couple of times but hasn't made contact with Phuong yet — I don't know what the hold-up is. But every time the phone rings, my father goes rigid. He's so tense, it's like he's expecting the worst," Quyen explained.

"Well, after all these years of wondering and trying to find out what happened, I guess anyone could be expected to feel a little stressed out, don't you think?"

"I suppose," Quyen agreed reluctantly. "But I really miss my mother. I just wish she'd find her niece, catch up on the last twenty-five years, and come back home! I guess that sounds selfish, doesn't it?"

"Quyen Ha, selfish?" Amelie exclaimed. "That'll be the day!"

How in the world is it, Quyen asked herself once again, *that my friends don't see how truly flawed I am?*

16

Getting There

January, already a short school month, was packed with activity at Nellie McClung Middle School. The two, huge, five-day volleyball tournaments, one for the girls and one for the boys, kept many McClung students and teachers occupied for twelve-hour days. But the events were so much fun and did so much for school spirit that no one objected, and the time, because everyone was having fun, flew by. In the girls' tournament, the Cougars made it to the finals, but lost in the third set to the powerful Bliss Carman team from Scarborough.

"Oh, well," Amelie had sighed. "At least we still have our own board championships next month. I'm sure we'll do well there."

"You will!" Quyen had agreed with certainty. Amelie's eternal optimism was contagious. "I didn't see any local teams at our tournament who would give you any trouble."

Quyen's mother still had not returned from Vietnam by the time the basketball regional club championships rolled around at the end of the month. Quyen and Ming missed their mother terribly, but her news was good. She had finally met with Phuong and established without any doubt that Phuong was, indeed, her long-lost niece. Mrs. Ha was expected home any day now.

The Shooting Stars played six games in January and won four of them. One of the losses occurred when Quyen was required to write her Vietnamese school exam. Her father would not hear of excusing her. The other loss had been in a very close game that Anna and two other players had missed because of a bad case of the flu.

"So we ended up in second place, girls," Coach Andrews explained to the team at their last Wednesday practice before the tournament. "It's a little disappointing, for sure, because I know that when everybody's healthy, we're the best team in our division."

"Don't look so gloomy!" Pauline scolded the team. "If we win both our preliminary games this Friday and Saturday, we'll still be in a good position to meet Gloucester in the finals on Sunday."

"It means we need to beat Almonte this time. They're in our pool," Coach Andrews added. Almonte was the team the Stars had lost to the day Anna ended up getting suspended from the team.

"We will, Coach," Katie said. "We're not the same team we were when we played them last." She looked at Quyen, who nodded her agreement.

"Well, that's the attitude we need," Pauline pointed out. "Now let's see some energy at this practice!"

* * *

"When is she going to get here?" Amelie demanded, looking out Quyen's living-room window.

Friday arrived, the first night of the regional championship tournament, and the girls were waiting for Pauline to pick them up. The Stars' game was at seven o'clock against the Kanata Cavaliers, a team they had beaten easily earlier in the season.

"Relax, Ammi, it's only six o'clock," Quyen replied patiently, checking her bag to make sure she had everything.

"Yeah, but you've got to get there, change, and warm up!" Amelie insisted.

"Right, and the school is, like, ten minutes ..." Quyen replied.

"Here she is!" Amelie interrupted. "Come on."

"Jeez, Ammi, you'd think *you* were the one who was playing," Quyen said with a grin.

"Well, one of us has to be excited." Amelie said as the girls pulled on their jackets and stepped into big winter boots.

"What makes you think I'm not excited?" Quyen demanded, a little indignant.

"You're, like, ho-hum, just another game. Big deal."

"No, I'm not," Quyen replied, "I just don't show it as much as you."

"No kidding," said Amelie as they got into the back of Pauline's car.

They arrived at the host high school fifteen minutes later. A light sleet was falling and Pauline drove extra cautiously.

After changing into her black and white Shooting Stars uniform, Quyen joined some of her teammates taking shots and loosely warming up. At six-thirty, the team began their regular pre-game warm-up even though Anna had not yet arrived. By six-forty-five, the players and their coaches were concerned when there was still no sign of her.

"What do you think's happened?" Amelie asked when Quyen came over to the bleachers to tell her about the missing player.

"No idea," Quyen shrugged. "She was fine at Wednesday's practice. She seemed to be pumped for this tournament."

Coach Andrews called the team to the bench five minutes before the start of the game to advise them of changes in the game plan due to Anna's absence. "There are two mental adjustments you have to make now," he told the team. "First, don't take this team for granted just because we beat them before. Any team can be beaten on any given day if they don't respect the opponent. Secondly, the Stars have no stars. We're a team and we're capable of success with any combination of players on the court. Any player who thinks we have to have Anna here to win this game, speak up now. You can watch the game from the bench."

No one said a word.

Anna did not show up until the last quarter. Fortunately, the team had the game well in hand by then, as the rules did not permit her to start playing at that point in the game.

"Where have you been?" the girls on the bench demanded when Anna joined them. She was as white as a ghost and Quyen noticed that she looked kind of shaky.

"We had an accident," Anna replied, her usual cool demeanor abandoned. "The Queensway was like a skating rink. Someone ran into us from behind and pushed us into the car ahead. By the time the chain reaction was over, there were fifteen cars piled up."

It was time for the players to go back on the floor for the last five minutes. Quyen put a hand on Anna's shoulder briefly. "I'm glad you're not hurt. Don't worry about the game. We missed you, but we're doing okay," she said before running onto the floor. Quyen realized that it was probably the most she'd ever said to Anna.

Amelie spent the night at Quyen's, and the next morning they returned to the same school for the other preliminary game against Almonte. This time Quyen's father drove them, excusing Ming from Vietnamese school so she could come along as well. Mr. Ha was in unusually good spirits, and the fact that he was coming to watch her play was thrilling for Quyen. Up until then, her parents had shown no interest in sports, preferring more intellectual pursuits.

The Stars and their coaches were grateful that all twelve players showed up this time and were in good health. The game was tough, mentally and physically, and at halftime the Stars were down by seven points.

"This game isn't over, girls," Coach Andrews said with confidence. "Don't give it to them for nothing! Let's go into a three-two zone defense and see if we can stop some of those layups. When you're even, we'll go back to one-on-one. Anna, don't let number five bully you in the post."

Quyen cringed inwardly at the unintended irony of Coach Andrews words, although Anna seemed to have given up her bullying ways, at least as far as Quyen could tell.

The tide turned in the second half. The zone defense frustrated the Almonte team and they started taking bad shots. Anna held her ground better in the post and, by the last quarter, the score was even.

With eight minutes to go, the team from Almonte unravelled and the Stars pulled off an eight-point victory.

"Okay," Coach Andrews said, trying to calm his excited team, "you've got to try and stay focussed. We have a quarterfinal game this afternoon against Hawkesbury. If we win that, it's on to a semi-final tomorrow morning."

"Quyen," Mr. Ha said when they'd settled into a booth at Pizza Palace for lunch, "I cannot say I understand this game. But I can tell that you know what you're doing when you play it. I am proud of you."

"Thank you," Quyen said quietly.

"Quyen is the most important player on the team, Father," Ming informed him. "In the position she plays, her responsibility is to decide what the team will do when they have the ball."

"Right," added Amelie. "And nobody does that better than Quyen!"

Quyen cleared her throat, signalling her discomfort with the direction of the conversation. "When will Mother be home?" she asked, changing the topic.

"If all her connections are smooth, she should arrive tomorrow afternoon. I will stay in communication with the airlines throughout the day," Mr. Ha replied. Quyen was sure there was a sparkle in his eye as he anticipated his wife's return. Quyen knew that both she and Ming were very eager to see their mother again.

* * *

On Sunday morning, Quyen was once again awaiting a ride with Pauline to the tournament. The Stars had played an outstanding game versus Hawkesbury in the quarter-final on Saturday afternoon and had defeated the speedy team with surprising ease. Their semi-final game would be played at ten-thirty against the Kemptville Royals, the team they had lost to during the regular season when Quyen had not been available to play.

"Well, this game is our ticket to the big dance with Gloucester," Coach Andrews began. "The Badgers are playing their semi-final this morning at the same time over at St. Pete's."

"We should have won the game the last time we played Kemptville," Pauline said. "Now that we've got our whole team together, it should be a walk in the park." She grinned at Quyen. "That means 'easy.'"

But a walk in the park it wasn't. The Shooting Stars were not shooting stars at all in the first half. Everyone missed even the easiest shots. Luckily, the Royals weren't in top form either. The score was low, 22–14 in favour of their opponents, when the Ottawa team stepped off the court at halftime.

"Let's get in gear, girls," Coach Andrews implored. "You've got to start making shots."

Little by little, basket by hard-earned basket, the Stars clawed their way back into the game. Anna scored the winning basket with two seconds left on the clock, after grabbing the rebound from a missed three-point shot. The team was delirious. They would be going to the final that afternoon and they knew, without having to be told, that they would be facing the Gloucester Badgers.

17

Shooting Stars

Coach Andrews spent the next two hours trying to keep his Shooting Stars focussed. Quyen sensed that the team was evenly divided between those who felt a little intimidated at the prospect of facing the Badgers again and those who relished the opportunity. As for herself, she was having difficulty concentrating on basketball when her mother, who had been gone for more than three weeks, would possibly be returning later that day.

Amelie had not been able to come to the morning game because of a family obligation, but Quyen phoned her after the semi-final victory and Amelie's father said he'd bring her to the big game. When she spoke to her own father, Mr. Ha reassured her that so far, everything seemed to be on schedule. If she came in on time, Mr. Ha would bring his wife and Ming to see the last part of the game.

Despite her distraction, Quyen settled down quickly once the warm-up began.

In line to shoot layups, Anna said to Quyen from behind, "Let's really try to do it this time. You know, for the sake of the team."

Quyen thought she knew what it must take for Anna to initiate such a pact. Very few words had passed between them since the big revelation about Anna's father. But they were playing well together and, although their relationship was not particularly friendly, Quyen no longer sensed the seething hatred of their previous interactions.

Quyen turned to respond. "Let's not 'try.' Let's just do it!"

Anna nodded her agreement and stuck out her hand, which Quyen swiped in a high five.

Quyen saw Amelie enter the gym with her father. She waved at them, happy that there would be a small cheering section there for her.

After their coaches had given them last-minute instructions and reminders, the starters ran out to the middle of the court, taking their positions on the circle.

The game was a battle from the first jump ball. The Badger coach badgered his players relentlessly from the sideline and his finely tuned machine performed like basketball robots, every player knowing exactly where every teammate was and where she would go. The Gloucester team had earned their reputation as a Goliath-like opponent honestly, and the Stars worked feverishly to stay with them.

Quyen, introspective and quiet by nature, was transformed, a captain calling out commands to her troops. "Neptune!" she cried, identifying the play she wanted to run. The effort and desire to triumph was etched on the face of each and every Shooting Star.

Nevertheless, the Badgers maintained a small lead throughout the first half and were up by three at halftime.

"Good work, girls," Pauline said as they came to the bench.

"You're hanging in with them," Coach Andrews said in agreement. "But this is it. Two more eight-minute quarters. We have to make a move soon."

The players nodded.

"Quyen, your three-point shot has improved a lot in the last few weeks. Why don't you try one if you get the opportunity?" Coach Andrews continued. "They're not showing us any respect on the perimeter. Anna, you and Katie have got to really crash the boards and go right back up. If nothing else, you might get fouled and take free throws. We've got to start taking some risks."

"Just remember," Pauline said, "you've got something going for you that they don't — heart."

"It's time to dig down deep now, girls," Coach Andrews concluded.

Back out on the floor, Quyen took the inbound pass from Katie and started dribbling towards the top of the key. Her defender mirrored her every move, backpedalling in the direction Quyen was heading. Suddenly, at the three-point line Quyen pulled up, eyed the back of the rim, and released a rainbow shot that dropped straight through the net without touching the rim. For the first time in the game, the Stars were tied with the Badgers.

The team responded to this feat by redoubling their efforts on both offense and defense. The Badger coach was frantic on the sideline. He signalled for a time out.

"He's trying to prevent us from getting any momentum going," Coach Andrews explained back at the bench. "So why don't you just do it again, Quyen?"

And she did. For the first time, members of the Gloucester team wore expressions on their faces. Some were angry, others simply frustrated. Their coach never stopped yelling at them. On her next possession, Quyen was not surprised to have her defensive player cover her at the three-point line. Quyen faked a pass to the other guard, then fired the ball overhead to Anna who was flashing to the top of the key. Quyen stepped around her defender and brushed by Anna, who flipped her the ball, which Quyen then took to the hoop for an uncontested layup.

Mercilessly harassed by their coach, the Badgers were nevertheless unable to regain their previous momentum and, when it was over, the Ottawa Shooting Stars had defeated the mighty Gloucester Badgers by a score of 47–35, and were the new Eastern Ontario champions. The Stars jumped up and down and hugged each other and jumped up and down again. Pauline was right in the middle of it while Coach Andrews watched from the sideline, a big smile on his face.

Then Quyen spotted them. Her father was in the first row of the bleachers, clapping in his dignified way. Ming stood, cheering, on one side of him. She saw her mother and, between her parents, a young woman who was also on her feet applauding. And at last she knew the secret, the information she'd been so sure had been left unsaid.

She broke away from her celebrating teammates and walked slowly towards her family. She continued to stare at the young woman who was supposed to be her cousin. But it was herself, an older version of herself. And she knew at that moment that this was not her cousin.

It was her sister.

Epilogue

The Shooting Stars were celebrating their championship with a party at the following Wednesday's practice. They had achieved the goal they'd set for themselves and had done a thorough job of it. The coaches and parents contributed food and drinks, and the players brought their favourite CDs with the intention of dancing and singing. But what the girls ended up doing was playing basketball. They had a quick game for fun, then started in on the refreshments.

When the specially ordered cake was cut, Quyen took her piece and went to one of the benches.

"Mind if I join you?" Anna asked.

Quyen looked at her. Anna's cheeks were flushed. *She's nervous,* Quyen thought to herself. "Have a seat," she said.

They ate their cake in silence for a couple minutes, then Anna spoke. "Quyen, would it be rude if I asked you what happened there after the game on Sunday with you and your family? You looked like someone who'd seen a ghost."

Quyen thought about what to say in response. She looked at Anna and recalled the emotionally painful upbringing and the loss of a father that this girl had endured. And she decided to tell Anna a story.

"I have recently learned some astonishing things about my family," she began quietly.

Seeing Anna nod her head in interest, Quyen continued. "When my parents lived in Vietnam, my father was married to another woman before my mother. His wife was my mother's older sister. Near the end of the war, my father, his wife and her younger sister were in a refugee camp. My father and his wife had a baby daughter." Quyen stopped for a moment to reflect. She glanced at Anna and saw that she had her full attention.

"During a raid on the camp my father became separated from his wife and child. When he was evacuated and eventually came to Canada, only his wife's younger sister was with him. My father and mother tried for years to learn the fate of their loved ones, without success.

"After working and putting himself through university, my father worked hard and saved enough money to buy a business while continuing to take care of his wife's sister. Then, after several years that still brought no information about my father's wife and child, my father and mother married and had a family. Last summer, my father finally received confirmation that his first wife had died in the refugee camp, but the whereabouts of his child were unknown."

Anna's eyes were huge and moist as she listened to Quyen's story, her face spellbound.

Quyen continued. "Finally, a few weeks ago my parents received word that the child, now a woman of course, had been located, so my mother went to Vietnam to confirm her identity. When she had done that, arrangements were made to bring my half-sister here with my mother for a visit. We will now apply for her to immigrate to Canada and live with us."

When Quyen stopped speaking, a cloud of respectful silence hung in the air between the two girls. Anna, crying softly, whispered, "I thought I was the only one ..." She sniffed, then took a deep breath. "But think about it, Quyen. You and I have both been touched in terrible ways by a war that ended way before we were born, a war that took place on the other side of the world. Isn't it amazing?"

Quyen could only nod her head. It *was* amazing. Amazing and wonderful, too, to have found a sister she never knew existed. The Shooting Star smiled, and, for the first time in years, she allowed her own tears to fall.

Other books you'll enjoy in the Sports Stories series ...

Baseball

☐ *Curve Ball* by John Danakas #1
Tom Poulos is looking forward to a summer of baseball in Toronto until his mother puts him on a plane to Winnipeg.

☐ *Baseball Crazy* by Martyn Godfrey #10
Rob Carter wins an all-expenses-paid chance to be batboy at the Blue Jays spring training camp in Florida.

☐ *Shark Attack* by Judi Peers #25
The East City Sharks have a good chance of winning the county championship until their arch rivals get a tough new pitcher.

☐ *Hit and Run* by Dawn Hunter and Karen Hunter #35
Glen Thomson is a talented pitcher, but as his ego inflates, team morale plummets. Will he learn from being benched for losing his temper?

Basketball

☐ *Fast Break* by Michael Coldwell #8
Moving from Toronto to small-town Nova Scotia was rough, but when Jeff makes the school basketball team he thinks things are looking up.

☐ *Camp All-Star* by Michael Coldwell #12
In this insider's view of a basketball camp, Jeff Lang encounters some unexpected challenges.

☐ *Nothing but Net* by Michael Coldwell #18
The Cape Breton Grizzly Bears prepare for an out-of-town basketball tournament they're sure to lose.

☐ *Slam Dunk* by Steven Barwin and Gabriel David Tick #23
In this sequel to *Roller Hockey Blues*, Mason Ashbury's basketball team adjusts to the arrival of some new players: girls.

Figure Skating

Gymnastics

Ice Hockey

☐ *Two Minutes for Roughing* by Joseph Romain #2
As a new player on a tough Toronto hockey team, Les must fight to fit in.

☐ *Hockey Night in Transcona* by John Danakas #7
Cody Powell gets promoted to the Transcona Sharks' first line, bumping out the coach's son, who's not happy with the change.

☐ *Face Off* by C. A. Forsyth #13
A talented hockey player finds himself competing with his best friend for a spot on a select team.

☐ *Hat Trick* by Jacqueline Guest #20
The only girl on an all-boy hockey team works to earn the captain's respect and her mother's approval.

☐ *Hockey Heroes* by John Danakas #22
A left-winger on the thirteen-year-old Transcona Sharks adjusts to a new best friend and his mom's boyfriend.

☐ *Hockey Heat Wave* by C. A. Forsyth #27
In this sequel to *Face Off*, Zack and Mitch encounter some trouble when it looks like only one of them will make the select team at hockey camp.

☐ *Shoot to Score* by Sandra Richmond #31
Playing defense on the B list alongside the coach's mean-spirited son is a tough obstacle for Steven to overcome, but he perseveres and changes his luck.

☐ *Brothers on Ice* by John Danakas #44
Brothers Dylan and Deke both want to play goal for the same team.

☐ *Rookie Season* by Jacqueline Guest #42
What happens when a boy wants to join an all-girl hockey team?

Riding

☐ *A Way with Horses* by Peter McPhee #11
A young Alberta rider invited to study show jumping at a posh, local riding school uncovers a secret.

☐ *Riding Scared* by Marion Crook #15
A reluctant new rider struggles to overcome her fear of horses.

☐ *Katie's Midnight Ride* by C. A. Forsyth #16
An ambitious barrel racer finds herself without a horse weeks before her biggest rodeo.

☐ *Glory Ride* by Tamara L. Williams #21
Chloe Anderson fights memories of a tragic fall for a place on the Ontario Young Riders Team.

☐ *Cutting It Close* by Marion Crook #24
In this novel about barrel racing, a talented young rider finds her horse is in trouble just as she is about to compete in an important event.

☐ *Shadow Ride* by Tamara L. Williams #37
Bronwen has to choose between competing aggressively for herself or helping out a teammate.

Roller Hockey

☐ *Roller Hockey Blues* by Steven Barwin
and Gabriel David Tick #17
Mason Ashbury faces a summer of boredom until he makes the roller-hockey team.

Running

☐ *Fast Finish* by Bill Swan #30
Noah is a promising young runner headed for the provincial finals when he suddenly decides to withdraw from the event.

Sailing

☐ *Sink or Swim* by William Pasnak #5
Dario can barely manage the dog paddle, but thanks to his mother
he's spending the summer at a water sports camp.

Soccer

☐ *Lizzie's Soccer Showdown* by John Danakas #3
When Lizzie asks why the boys and girls can't play together, she
finds herself the new captain of the soccer team.

☐ *Alecia's Challenge* by Sandra Diersch #32
Thirteen-year-old Alecia has to cope with a new school, a new
stepfather and friends who have suddenly discovered the opposite
sex.

☐ *Shut-Out!* by Camilla Reghelini Rivers #39
David wants to play soccer more than anything, but will the new
coach let him?

☐ *Offside!* by Sandra Diersch #43
Alecia has to confront a new girl who drives her fellow teammates
crazy.

☐ *Heads Up!* by Dawn Hunter and Karen Hunter #45
Do the Warriors really need a new, hot-shot player who skips
practice?

Swimming

☐ *Breathing Not Required* by Michele Martin Bossley #4
Gracie works so hard to be chosen for the solo at synchronized
swimming that she almost loses her best friend in the process.

☐ *Water Fight!* by Michele Martin Bossley #14
Josie's perfect sister is driving her crazy but when she takes up
swimming — Josie's sport — it's too much to take.

☐ *Taking a Dive* by Michele Martin Bossley #19
Josie holds the provincial record for the butterfly, but in this
sequel to *Water Fight!*, she can't seem to match her own time and
might not go on to the nationals.

☐ *Great Lengths* by Sandra Diersch #26
Fourteen-year-old Jessie decides to find out whether the rumours about a new swimmer at her Vancouver club are true.

☐ *Pool Princess* by Michele Martin Bossley #47
In this sequel to *Breathing Not Required*, Gracie must deal with a bully on the new synchro team that she joins in Calgary.

Track and Field

☐ *Mikayla's Victory* by Cynthia Bates #29
Mikayla must compete against her friend if she wants to represent her school at an important track event.